Dragons Are People, Too

Way Beyond the Sky, Where Dragons Rule, Volume 2

Jeri Andrew

Published by Jeri Andrew, 2023.

This is a work of fiction. Similarities to real people, places, or events are entirely coincidental.

DRAGONS ARE PEOPLE, TOO

First edition. September 14, 2023.

Copyright © 2023 Jeri Andrew.

ISBN: 979-8223710189

Written by Jeri Andrew.

Table of Contents

To Drew. Without you, there would be no series to be enjoyed! Thank you for your support through the project! You're the greatest!

Volume 2: Dragons Are People, Too

Chapter 1

Keithen was scratching his head, pacing...

He just didn't quite know what to make of it all.

Life could sure be confusing.

Keithen knew his egg had laid dormant for half a century, due to a quake that occurred while his family was away on vacation.

Fortunately, his egg had rolled, landing in a bed of silver moss by the straight face base of the mountain. Luckily, a flat slab fell first, landing at an angle, creating a tomb, once tons of rock and dirt slid down and buried him. (Dragon eggs will lay dormant, unless it's able to draw nutrients from a parent, or other creature).

What he wasn't clear about, was why it took so many years for George to find him.

Oh, the young prince was grateful that his father never gave up looking for him, but he hadn't really thought about the details much.

His poor mother, believing her husband to have died when an aftershock sent tons of rock and dirt down on top of him.

What none of them realized, except George, of course, was that George had shifted, in order to crawl through a small cave opening he found while digging, then the aftershock struck. Human miners found him, nearly dead. When he woke up, he couldn't remember anything, not even his name, or, that he's a dragon, much less remembering that he was the king of Drakonia! King of the world!

Barbara was his nurse. She was very kind, as well as devoted. She remained by his side both day and night until he woke up from his coma.

Barbara continued to take care of George, calling him John, John Doe, until he was pretty much healed.

The two of them fell in love. Once John was stronger, he took a job in a quarry. Soon after, he proposed to Barbara.

To the best of George's knowledge, no one had ever come looking for him, so, John began a whole new life for himself.

Years passed since Barbara had begun taking care of John.

One day, while John was at work, digging in the quarry, a small quake shook the ground, causing a minor rock slide.

George stood up straight, all of a sudden, his memory came flooding back!

He began to run to the other side of the mountain, stopped and shifted for the first time in decades! Then took to the skies, flying back to search for Keithen's lost egg.

He had a whole new motivation for finding that egg!

As long as he had been gone, and, in light of his second life, he dared not return to Isabel without that egg!

The king worked day and night, digging with a whole new energy, relentless in his pursuit for at least a remnant of that egg!

The day finally arrived!

George couldn't believe his eyes when he saw the pocket created by that leaning shelf.

But, there laid Keithen's egg, safe and sound, on that bed of silver moss!

He thanked the powers that be, tucked the egg safely away in his pouch and headed back home to his Queen, his love, his wife, his life!

He hadn't even given Barbara a second thought.

Poor Barbara never knew what became of John. He left for work one day and just never returned!

They had had such a good life together! She had planned to tell him that they were expecting, over a romantic dinner for 2 that evening, when he got home from work. She never got the chance, raising her son alone, and at her age. A son she had hoped would bind her and John together, forever. She knew the day would come that he would remember who he was. Her son was to be her insurance that they would always be connected. Only, she didn't get the chance to tell him!

She loved her son very much and raised him as best she could, keeping his identity a secret as much as possible. She assumed John memory had returned, she wasn't wrong. Barbara was afraid for her life! Fearing that with the return of his memory, he might actually order her execution.

When George first landed back home, a crowd quickly gathered to greet the returning king, long sense thought to be dead.

He was told about Isabel remarrying, having a son and her new husband also disappearing.

His heart broke for his poor wife, but, he didn't feel quite as guilty about Barbara.

He swore everyone to secrecy, so that he could surprise Isabel, then rushed home.

The anxious king opened the door to their home, trying to use humor to lighten the blow, he hollered, "Honey, I'm Home!"

Isabel took one look at George and passed smooth out!

She woke up to George holding her in his arms.

"Sweetheart, it's me, honey, I'm home and look, I found our egg!" he pulled the egg from his pouch and showed it to her. She passed out again!

When she woke up, she was laying in her bed with George fast asleep beside her.

Isabel was in shock! George felt her stirring and woke up. He told her that he knew all about her son and there was nothing to be forgiven for... she had done nothing wrong.

He apologized profusely for having been gone so long and told her he had been in an accident, losing his memory, but didn't exactly fill in the details.

The expectant dad carried their egg to hatch, named him Prince Keithen and restarted their family with 2 sons.

Braynar was 11 years old. A very tender age... when a boy really needs a father! He and George bonded right away and life went on.

Keithen had never really given any thought to who Braynar's father was, neither had Braynar. As far as the boys were concerned, George was dad..

Now, they find out that Mother was married again while she thought herself to be a widow, then lost her second husband. They felt really badly for everything their mother had endured. They had a whole new respect for her.

"DANALLI , DUDE, THERE'S a human woman looking for you, says she's your mother!" Craigen said to his long time friend. Danalli had never really spoken of his mother to anyone... it wasn't that he was ashamed of her, or of her being human, he didn't really know how he felt, or how the other dragons would feel, if they knew he was also human.

"Yeah, okay, thanks man, um, um, well um, yeah, show her in," He said nervously, as he quickly shifted.

It had been ages since he'd seen his mother.

"Danalli!

My baby!"

"Hello mother, it's so good to see you!" He said, then picked her up for a big hug.

"You've really grown, filled out, look how muscular you are as a man!

Wow, son!

Look at you!

I heard you were badly injured saving the planet from horrid aliens and were barely clinging to life, so, I rushed here as fast as I could get here!

It's not so easy to find anyone willing to come to Drakonia on purpose and I'm getting old."

"Well, you look great, mom!

Ya, the battle really zapped me, but I recovered quickly and am feeling fine, now. Ready to fight again, if need be.

Mom, I was about to go see the King, come, go with me and I will request some time off so you and I can get all caught up," Danalli said to his mom.

"Sure, do I look alright to meet royalty?" She asked

"Mother, you look fine!

Beautiful as always!"

"You're a good son Danalli," his mother remarked.

"Your majesty, Danalli and his mother are here to see you," Thomlin announced.

"His mother? Well, show them in, don't just stand there!"

"John!" Barbara said with a look of shock on her face.

"Barbara?" George said, in total disbelief.

"John?" Isabel asked, then said, "No, this is King George."

"King?" Barbara asked.

"Uh, well, uh, you see, Isabel, Sweetheart, when I was rescued from the rock slide, I was in human state and was I suffering from amnesia when I woke up from a coma. Barbara here was my nurse.

After some time, We fell in love and we got married. But then, there was this quake, I was at work moving rocks, when I remembered! I remembered everything! I rushed back to the spot where I knew our son's egg was buried... I began digging until I found our son and I flew back to you... Barbara I'm so sorry! I didn't mean to leave without a word! So I see you got on with your life and remarried, as well as had a child... that's wonderful! I didn't know Danalli was your son."

"George, I did not remarry.

Danalli is our son!

I was going to tell you at dinner that night, but you never came home!

You just vanished!"

Danalli was in shock! "You're my dad?"

"You're my son?!?!?!!"

Isabel spoke up, "No George, He's your First Born Son! Just as Braynar is my first born son. Prince Danalli, heir to the throne of Drakonia...

And...

He is half human.

George, don't you realize, he fulfills prophecy. The king that would unite Dragon kind with humans. The king that would bring peace between the two sides ... but not without incidents."

"The king?" Danalli said.

"Now Isabel let's don't get ahead of ourselves.

We don't know that he's the prophesied king, we only know that he's part human.

The rest remains to be seen... don't be putting things in the man's head that don't belong." George cautioned his lovely wife.

"George, you're still married to Barbara! She is still your wife!"Isabel said as she used her magic to produce a crown and change Barbara's clothing to those of a queen.

Barbara stood there, in shock, not quite knowing what to say, as did Danalli.

Isabel broke the stunned silence," Barbara, you will stay here, in Drakonia, and take your rightful place on your throne, right next to mine.

I, am a born Queen, a Reining Queen, you, are a married Queen as well as mother to the future king.

Married queens are not necessarily reining queens, however, you are to be treated with the same respect, the respect due the wife of a king and mother of a future king."

"We are all going to live together? " She asked, wondering how that would all work out. Then, Raynar walked into the room.

George thought it best to call for a family meeting, followed by a public address....

"Your majesties, Queen AlaHanDrea is here to see you.," Craigen announced.

"Good, she needs to hear this as well," Isabel said.

Once the meeting was over, AlaHanDrea shocked everyone by spinning a cocoon around Barbara! Once the woman was fully entombed, AlaHanDrea looked at them and said, "y'all worry entirely too much!" A short time later, AlaHanDrea slowly opened the cocoon.

A very young looking Barbara stepped out...

AlaHanDrea addressed the group, "how can y'all expect her to live with y'all, here in Drakonia,, as a feeble, fragile, old human female? It would surely kill her! I just did her a big favor and changed her a little.

Ok, so, I changed her a lot...

I evened the playing field a bit for her.

Now, she doesn't have to die so young, or age so quickly.

I gave her part of me."

"Oh child! You beautiful, marvelous child! I love you, child! Thank you, thank you so much!" Barbara said.

"Fair is fair, Queen Barbara! The way it was, wasn't fair! You were too old! You were cheated out of irreplaceable years! So, I sort of replaced them and gave you more.

I could, so I did.

It's a gift... I hope you make the most out of it.

Just so you'll know, barring any accidents, you should live for about as long as I will. I... I live longer than Dragons do!

Well, except for My dragons, I forbid them to die, at least until after I do."

Stunned silence filled the room!

AlaHanDrea broke the silence, "nice of y'all to tell me that you're dragons. I just love finding out this way. I would have never guessed... okay, so, Danalli, are you the dragon I rode in the battle?"

"Yes, tiny one, I am."

AlaHanDrea fluttered over, landing on Danalli's shoulder and took a seat.

"Just so all y'all know, I detest secrets. So, let's try to not let this happen again. This thing about keeping secrets from me." She said, feeling very irritated.

AlaHanDrea looked at Barbara and said, "oh, one more thing, you can now do some magic and stuff. By giving you part of myself, you are part me.

Let me show you what I mean. See that Boulder over there? Stare at it real hard and think, blow up."

Barbara did as instructed and the boulder exploded into dust!

"Now, Stare at it and think, go back together."

Barbara couldn't believe what she had just done!

"Okay, now, point away from everyone, think, Freeze and blow really hard."

Barbara did as instructed and blew frozen flames!

"Wow! Oh wow!" She exclaimed.

"That's only the tip of the iceberg, hold your arms out to your side and flex your back muscles..."

Wings appeared on Barbara's back!

They weren't huge like a dragons wings, they were like the baby girls wings, meant for fluttering around. She tried them out, laughing and having the time of her life!

AlaHanDrea had the biggest grin on her face! She was very proud of herself.

Everyone in the room had smiles on their faces.

"Baby girl, you are incredible!" Danalli said and everyone else agreed, praising her for the gift she had given to Barbara.

Chapter 2

The air had a strange coolness to it that had everyone feeling perplexed.

The reason for it soon materialized, when a thunderstorm began brewing, much to the astonishment of everyone around.

AlaHanDrea got very excited! She headed for high ground and took position.

Her dragons were confused as to why she had flown out to greet it... until...

Lightening began to strike and thunder began to rumble. AlaHanDrea held her arms up high, tilted her head back, face to the sky and began to sing very loudly. All of a sudden, lightening bolts began striking the tiny girl!

Everyone on the ground felt horrified!

Only the lightening didn't seem to be bothering her in a negative way!

They all looked on, while she absorbed lightning bolt after lightning bolt, swelling in size! Seeming to pull the storm into herself!

When she was done, she let out a thunderous scream that shook the ground! Then squatted down and peed a stream!

Afterwards, she burped and said, "Scuse me," then giggled, just like she always did.

"Did y'all see what I just saw?

That baby girl just ate a thunderstorm!

She ate a freaking thunderstorm!" King George exclaimed!

"What Is She?" Barbara asked, in shock of what she had just seen.

"She's a one of a kind, that's what she is, And... she's from Ion 6, a research Moon, some 9 billion light years from here... Before it exploded from 2 galaxies colliding," Danalli explained.

Ground fog appeared with a bright light. Not as bright as if it were God, but bright, just the same.

"Fear not, it's just me..." He was interrupted by AlaHanDrea.

"Mitchin! Mitchin! Oh Mitchin! He's My Angel! Oh, Mitchin, it's So good to see you!" She squealed, as she rushed over to hug his neck.

"It's good to see you as well, baby girl. Sorry it took me so long. I had to cancel my vacation for a short time while everyone got resettled. But, I'm back on vacation!"

"Everybody, I want to meet my angel, Mitchin! He is the one that came and told me my name after I got born!" She told them proudly.

"Mitchin, this is King George, Queen Isabel, Queen Barbara, TeeHeeHee, King Raynar you already know, Prince Danalli, Prince Keithen, Prince Braynar and Paulio, Paulio is a royal guard." AlaHanDrea said, making all of the appropriate introductions.

"It's very nice to meet all of you," Mitchin told them.

Barbara looked at Mitchin, stunned. "You're a real angel?"

"Yes, your majesty, I am an angel, a real, angel. I'm here on vacation at the moment."

"Wow! Wow! I met a real angel! Wow! Angels are really real! Wow!"

"Yes ma'am, we are really real." Mitchin told her.

"Well, that means that.... Oh, that... " Barbara ran into the nearby cave.

Mitchin knew what she was doing, so he spoke up before anyone could interrupt her. "This is a normal response. Please, let her have her moments. She ran off to go pray. I see this happen often with humans. Once they see beyond all doubt that God is really real, they go to speak to Him. She's also embarrassed, she knows that I see her and all of her imperfections."

Everyone accepted his explanation and allowed Barbara her privacy.

"Well, she's had long enough, she's ready for some Heavenly intervention. I know this, because the big guy just told me so ..." Mitchin headed into the cave to speak with Barbara...

He found her laying in a heap on the ground, crying her eyes out. He scooped her up in his arms, materialized a double hammock and sat down with her in his arms. He looked deeply into her eyes until she smiled a little. "That's better, you're very pretty when you smile." He stayed beside her.

"Having faith isn't always easy. You'll no longer have those doubts.

He told me to tell you that you are forgiven.

You were forgiven before you even asked to be.

He loves you, ya know. Now, dry those tears.

He also told me to tell you that what AlaHanDrea did for you is not a sin, it's a blessed gift.

However, You are also forever part of her.

Don't be surprised if you feel her emotions or hear her thoughts from time to time."

"Mitchin, how long do dragons live?"

"Dragons have extremely long life spans, sometimes living for thousands of years. AlaHanDrea is a different story all together. We're not positive with her, but she will probably live in excess of 5,000 years!"

"So, I will live for more than 5,000 years? Oh wow! But if I don't want to live that long, what happens to me then?"

"Well, you get your head right about the fact that you're going to continue to live, and like it.

Try giving Glory to God. Use the time to better his kingdom. Just a suggestion?"

"You're right. Thank you for your time. May I ask you a question?"

"Sure, I'll even try to answer it," he joked.

"Vacation?"

"Yes, you see, there's this lady, this gorgeous, irresistible lady..."

"A lady, really? I didn't know that you guys..."

" We don't, unless we are on vacation, then we do! We very much do!"

"She's a very lucky woman."

"I'm not hers only. But, thank you. I'm on vacation. This is my flesh experience. I have no limits."

"Oh, I see."

Mitchin stood up, then took Barbara's hand and stood her up. He put his hands on her shoulders, gazed deeply into her eyes, tilted her chin up and kissed her, softly at first, then with more passion, before standing her back upright.

"Wow!" Was about all she could say, so, he kissed her again, longer that time. She melted in his arms.

"You are a very beautiful and desirable woman, Queen Barbara. Don't ever forget that or doubt that." He kissed her one more time, then excused himself. She sat back down, smiling.

AlaHanDrea was still outside of the cave, talking with Danalli, when Mitchin walked out.

"It's ok if you want to go in there, now, Danalli. She's fine, tho, she did just get kissed by an angel," he smiled and winked. Danalli smiled really big and shook Mitchin's hand, "it's good to meet you, Mitchin."

"Likewise, Danalli."

"Ooooh, you kissed Barbara!" the tiny queen teased.

"I sure did! And I liked it, too!" He teased right back.

Mermaids
In
The
Deep

Chapter 2

Mitchin was anxious to see Athena. He was hanging out with AlaHanDrea back at her place in her partially built tree house in Braynar and Keithen's front yard.

The tiny little elfen fairies were busy finishing building the tiny queens new home.

Mitchin was surprised that Athena hadn't been up to say hello to the baby girl and neither had Dane, yet.

He wasn't for certain they had made it through the tunnels yet. Neptune was in a different tunnel, so, he arrived at about the same time as AlaHanDrea did.

Time didn't exist inside the tunnels, so the precise time of landing, couldn't be accurately calculated.

Time is only relevant to a planet/orbiting object, revolving around it's central star.

Creatures were still arriving almost daily.

All arrivals were a mixture of species, due to the rush involved in the mass evacuation.

Still, AlaHanDrea missed Athena and Dane very much.

Mitchin was missing Athena, too.

The sound of rhythm drums signaled night approaching. Mitchin was beginning to really enjoy this part of living on Taurus 9.

AlaHanDrea took the cue from the drums to mean it was time for her to spin a good night cocoon.

Mitchin had been staying with the tiny queen, in her tree house. She loved having him there and he seemed to really enjoying being the grown up in her world.

For Mitchin, that was about the closest he'd come to raising a child.

Braynar and Keithen didn't seem to mind an angel living in their tree. They hardly even noticed, well, except for the fact that green things were greener, blooming things bloomed brighter and more plentifully...

A resident angel also seemed to keep bad things away.

Even Braynar used a different entrance when he went home drunk.

Being an angel seemed to be hindering Mitchin's social time, tho.

He knew that he was going to have to do something to make people loosen up around him.

AlaHanDrea must have been reading his thoughts, because she gave him a never empty barrel of her special nectar, then gave him a naughty wink and grin.

Then, she used her magic to change his clothing. She dressed him in a black button up shirt, halfway buttoned, sleeves rolled part way up, an open, black vest, black jeans and black boots.

She made sure the shirt showed off his muscles, as did the jeans. She re-combed his hair for him, too.

As a final touch, she used her magic to make a wagon for the nectar barrel, complete with disposable cups, with a dispenser that was never empty.

The wagon had sensors installed and would follow him around when he wanted it to.

"Very nice, baby girl. So, can you see my wings?" He asked her.

"Mitchin, you are what you are! You gotta make em love ya for partying, anyway!

Just go, have fun, be a little naughty, show them... You're on vacation!

And feed them my Special nectar, it makes folks say yes!"

She giggled.

"Thanks, sweetie, and you're right."

"Mitchin, holler at Danalli, Bray and Keithen, they kinda have the same problem, because they are royalty.

Oh, hey, I know, gather up the royals from Ion 6, plus our guys here, and Y'all throw a party very near their party and make it end up blending!"

"You're a genius! I love you so much, tiny girl! Sweet dreams baby girl."

"Thanks, now go, have some fun!"

The guys were not in their cave, so, Mitchin decided to just go to the party anyway.

Just as he'd feared, people began to act like children whose parents just came in the room. So, he walked over in front of the fire and asked for everyone to please hear him for a moment.

He had to levitate to get their attention.

"Hello everyone, my name is Mitchin and yes, I AM an angel. But, I'm not here in that capacity. Please don't treat me like an off duty police officer!

Angels get very few vacations, and this is my vacation.

My opportunity to be flesh.

I'm not expected to be perfect, and you sure don't have to be perfect around me!

I'm here to experience Life, just like you are.

I don't intend to commit any major sins, but there is a list of them I would like to commit!"

Laughter rose up. "Do y'all think you could assist me in getting down to some serious partying?

Maybe help me with my list?

So, Who Among you wants to corrupt an angel?

I brought Nectar!

Special Nectar!

Use with caution, sinful nectar!"

Applause rose up from the crowd!

Mitchin set himself down on the ground.

A beautiful red-haired woman asked him to dance. Of course, he agreed, as well as giving her some nectar to drink.

His nectar wagon stayed really busy all night long!

By the time Braynar and the guys arrived at the party, most folks were flying high on special nectar, dancing and having a great time! Some were having an extra good time and didn't care who watched!

It was wild times in the old town!

That was sure some powerful Nectar wine!

Keithen was the first one to fill a glass, but Bray was right behind him.

Danalli slipped away and went over to baby girl's camp.

He put up a hammock by her cocoon and laid down.

She wasn't really asleep. The sounds from the gathering were rather loud.

Ion 6 refugees began joining in and it just kept getting louder!

She unzipped her cocoon a little, "hello, Danalli. Thanks for sitting with me."

"I can't think of any place that I'd rather be. We haven't had much of a chance to talk, not with all of the drama going on."

"Ya, you've sure gone through some changes, for sure."

"That ain't no lie!" He agreed.

"I'm sorry I didn't talk to you first, before changing your mom."

"No, baby, it's o.k. I love what you did! You are so awesome for it! She looks great!"

"So, you're a prince and heir to the throne. How's it feel?"

"Very strange! I went from a single mother to 2 mom's and 2 dad's and all royalty! Oh ya, and 2 brothers! We will all sit on the thrones together and rule together some day. It's all so surreal."

"I can't think how that would be. Do you remember us being dead together?"

"Yes, I do. I'm also glad that I remember. That was some very special time. I'm so glad that your little fairy friends wouldn't allow us to cross over."

"Ya, me too!"

"Ya know, baby girl, I'm gonna marry you some day. Your Leon is going to have some serious competition, for real. So is Dane. I know, I'm third in line, but at least I'm in line! I fully intend to make you my wife someday!"

"Really? And you think that Leon and Dane think the same way?"

"Don't you? I realize that you're only 6, but you're not like most 6 year olds and you're very smart."

"Thank you. Ya, the line is a little bit longer... Neptune and Raynar longer... Maybe Braynar and Keithen longer... But, as fun as they all are, you and Leon are my 2.

I could not ever possibly choose.

I love you both too much to ever have to choose."

"Then I will never ask you to choose. I rather like your big kitty cat. For a lion, he's alright."

"Ya, he likes you, too."

"That never ending field of flowers was really special. We sure were dead a long time.

For a while there, I thought we would be staying there.

Truthfully, I could have stayed with you in that field of flowers for all of eternity if...

But, thanks to those fairies, here we are, and I get to watch you grow up, help you grow up... Make memories while you are growing up..."

"We're lucky, aren't we, Danalli?"

"Yes, baby girl, we are very fortunate."

"I love you, Danalli."

"I love you, too, baby girl!"

AlaHanDrea crawled out of her cocoon, fluttered over and kissed Danalli on his cheek, then fluttered over onto the ground. He watched her as she grew herself back to normal size.

"I didn't know you could make yourself bigger."

"I am this size naturally. I stay tiny to stay safe and so I don't end up having to kill someone for getting wrong with me. Please don't tell on me."

"You are so smart!"

"Thanks. Wanna see a neat trick?" She asked, then aged herself to 24!

A gorgeous, large breasted woman with a trim waist and rounded hip, shapely legs, long, full, curly hair and big green eyes stood before him, then shifted back to 6.

"That was a sneak peek."

"Wow! AlaHanDrea, wow! That's you all grown up?"

"Yes."

"Dayum! Girl! Oh! girl child! Yes ma'am, the day will come that you are my wife, my queen! Oh, that you were all grown up right now, today! I see that I am getting a good lesson in patience, here!

You sweet, precious girl.

I do look forward to the future with you!"

"And I, you, Danalli! We've already been dead together, I look forward to being alive together, too."

She crawled up in his lap and gave him a big hug. Then, she shrunk herself back down and put herself back in a cocoon, telling him to have sweet dreams and closed herself up in it.

Danalli used his magic to produce an instrument similar to a guitar. He made a small fire and began to play and sing for her while she went to sleep.

Danalli had such a beautiful voice! He sang quite a few songs to the baby girl while she slept in her cocoon.

What Danalli didn't realize, is that he had an audience.

Several young ladies were hiding behind a bush, watching and listening to that handsome, muscular man singing under the moonlight, lullabying a beautiful little baby girl while she slept in her cocoon.

When the ladies realized that he was through singing for the night, they allowed themselves to be known, motioning him to quietly come with them, which he did.

The rest of his night was one he would not soon forget!

He regretted the sun coming up when it did, but all good things must come to an end.

The ladies kissed him before leaving, giggling as they were walking down the path...

Danalli wasn't the only one with a night that was just now ending, because the sun came up.

Keithen and Braynar were pretty much carrying Mitchin back.

They laid him down in a hammock, then fell down, laughing.

Danalli joined them on the ground, feeling pretty tipsy his own self. They teased their brother about the small group of girls they saw leaving after having been with him... They all got a good laugh, then helped each other to the cave.

All of their caves branched off of the same Central cave, but each one had different entrances, too, that could be reached from the same entrance, if need be.

All three of them still ended up in the same spot, in three different beds in the same room.

All three of them quickly passed out, too.

Snoring could be heard all the way from the surface.

There wasn't a day go by that Ion 6 creatures didn't stop by to say hello to AlaHanDrea, as they arrived on Taurus 9, and that day was to be no different.

The guys had all just woken up, all hung over, crawling up out of the cave, when churning water indicated that company from the sea was arriving!

AlaHanDrea got so excited!

The guys looked up to see the most beautiful woman they had ever seen in their lives, emerging from the tiny pool that led from the sea.

She shed her fishtail for legs as she climbed out of the water. The guy's Jaws dropped and their eyes opened wide, as they looked at that beautiful creature!

The baby Queen was so excited, as was Athena! She no sooner got out of the water and changed to dry lander, then Dane came up out of the water as well.

The baby girl was so full of excitement she could barely contain herself!

Mitchin was still snoring in the hammock.

Athena shushed everyone, then went over and crawled in next to him.

When Mitchin woke up, he got so excited to see Athena that he accidentally flipped the hammock upside down!

Dane and the baby girl were locked in an embrace, so happy to see each other, they didn't want to let each other go. No one seemed to notice baby girl being normal size when she hugged Dane.

Chapter 3

Keithen, Braynar and Danalli were determined that this was the day for the "adults" in their lives, to sit and have a meaningful talk... answering many questions...

The boys were not without compassion. They made sure that the food wagon was plenty full. They also made sure there was plenty of human food available... for Barbara.

When the boys showed up at the parents cave, they were just getting up and around.

The boys served breakfast, then all sat down to listen while the "Adults" took turns telling their story, their way. They had time to prepare, and the boys were ready to actually listen and hear them.

Silently, all 3 of the sons sat and listened, while George told of how he'd first seen Isabel while she was still very young, vowing to meet her bride price once she came of age.

He told of how badly he longed for her to fall in love with him... how he believed that Keithen's egg was a key component that tied them together... once the egg was lost, George was convinced that he had to return with the egg if he wanted to please Isabel... how he could not abandon the search for his own child... how much Keithen meant to George, besides for Isabel... they listened as George described the horrors of the second avalanche, then the land slides that followed... about waking up and not remembering his own name...Being nursed back to health, but still not knowing who was before the avalanche...

he spoke of falling in love with the beautiful nurse that had taken such good care of him... He spoke of the day he suddenly remembered who he was as well as the quest he was on...he spoke of how he feverishly tore that pile of dirt and rocks to pieces for a few more years... he spoke of how by the time he made it back to see his Barbara, she had moved away... He spoke of returning to continue looking for the lost egg that was depending on its father to save it. He spoke of how time had no meaning until he finally, FINALLY found the egg, safe and sound, nestled safely on a bed of silver moss under the protection of a slab of slate that had slid down and leaned against the wall of the mountain, making a safe haven of protection against the falling dirt and rock... He spoke of how he tore ass back to Isabel... the joy of bringing the egg to hatch... he spoke of Braynar...

Isabel went next. She spoke about being a new bride, laying her first egg, the quake, the avalanche... losing her husband to the search for their egg, her guilt for putting him in harm's way to find the egg... she spoke of having to take over his duties as King... the lonely nights that stretched on forever... she spoke of Raynar coming to the rescue her when her thoughts turned to suicide...a new beginning, a new egg, but before she could tell Raynar about the egg, his dad sent him away for being disobedient. She spoke of raising Braynar and their years of just the two of them... she spoke of how Braynar gave her the strength to carry through after losing husband number 2. Then, she spoke of how one day, George came walking through the door with Keithen's egg in his pouch... and how she fainted...

Raynar spoke of how he'd also fallen in love with Isabel when she was very young. They had attended the same school for royals... He spoke of how his heart broke when George was first to meet the bride price... never realizing that other males were also trying to raise the price... Isabel was the daughter of the King! Her bride price was enormous!

He spoke of how he watched from a far, then how shocked he was that George vanished, presumed dead.

Fear prevented him from reaching out to her, he didn't want to come off as an opportunist... He spoke of feeling her deep sorrow and hearing a call in his head... a warning that she was going to try to end her own life, so she could reunite with her husband and lost egg on the other side, never realizing they were still alive. He spoke of how he rushed to her side, to let her know that she was not alone.

He spoke of how she remembered him from school, when he thought she never noticed him... he spoke of fearing his father would object to them marrying and decided not to tell his father until after the fact, hoping it would force the man to accept their marriage, only he was wrong and His father sent him away on assignment for being disobedient, before Isabel could tell him about their egg...

He spoke of the Joy and the pain of finding out that George had, indeed, survived the avalanche and returned home with their lost egg...

They listened to Barbara speak of finding George, saying she never knew who he really was, loving him, then losing him before getting to tell him that they were expecting... She spoke of the ridicule she received for having a baby, without a father for the baby and finally moved away when Danalli reached school age. She spoke of finding out that Danalli was half Dragon and capable of magic... How they had to move a lot when folks would learn their secret of Danalli being half dragon....

The boys were brothers. The three of them sat silently, not saying a single word. Their parents were all good and decent beings, powerful... royal... leaders... Together, the 4 of them were the parents of 3 fine, strong boys... love was present...compassion, understanding, forgiveness... acceptance...Isabell loved both of her husbands... George loved both of his wives...and so, it was one large household, at last... the 7 of them made a family...

Once the last story was told, all 3 boys got up and walked out without uttering a single word.

"Give them time, Isabel. They just need a little time to digest it all. We laid a lot on them," Raynar told the group.

"Raynar's right, they just need a little time," George agreed.

George hugged Raynar, Raynar patted Georges back…The women hugged.

Each man took a woman to hug then switched.

"We… We… Us 4, are a family. The children are add on's as well as no longer children. But us four, We, we are the core of the family. The ad ons are welcome members of this family, but we ARE the core!

Those boys are the results of our combined love for one another. We owe it to them to set a good example.

Now, while we are all here and speaking of this blended family, I'd like to bring up member number 8.

She may not be our blood, well, she IS Barbara's same DNA now… and, well, part of Raynar's as well, because she has Jax DNA… O.K., well, I suppose one could devise that Raynar and Barbara are her biological parents and they wouldn't really be wrong… or right… of course, she was pulled out of Jax, so technically, he could be classified as her mommy…"Everyone busted out laughing at that remark… "Like it or not, she is also a very real part of this family now. However, we are not to ever lose site of the fact that AlaHanDrea is an extremely dangerous creature. We are So lucky that she loves us! I, for one, never want her as an enemy!" they all agreed to that one!

"Personally, I think it's best to keep that young lady as close as possible. From what I've seen, she's more powerful than any creature known!" Raynar said. The worried look at Barbara's face said everything she was thinking.

"I can understand your worry, Barbara. We're not sure what she has instilled in you, by giving you part of herself… its a very generous gift, for sure! Especially the youth and longevity… but, I'd be willing to bet the girl would be more than happy to spend time with you to help you discover all that you are now capable of doing. In a sense, you were reborn a new creature, no longer 100% human, unique, a creature like none other, except of course, your 6 year old mother..." Isabel teased.

"DANALLI, DUDE, WAIT up," Braynar hollered out. "Wait up dude, I've got something for ya!"

"Sure, Bray, what's up, whatcha got?" Danalli responded.

"This box is for you, bro." Braynar handed his step brother the box he was holding.

"For me? it's not my birthday...Oh! Braynar! Bro! I, I, I don't know quite what to say! It's, it's, Wow, bro! Wow! It's Magnificent!" Danalli said.

"Well, go ahead, try it on, make sure it fits that big head of yours," Braynar teased.

"Braynar, WOW!" was Danalli seemed to be able to say.

"Well, you're a prince, are you not? And... A prince needs a fitting crown!"

"I never knew I was a prince.

I never guessed my true father is a king.

I never knew that I had brothers, especially not the very guys whose job it was to .... hey... wait... it just dawned on me... I LOST MY JOB!

I'm Unemployed!" They both busted out laughing at that one.

Keithen walked in, "The Crown looks great, Danalli!"

Braynar smiled and said, "Hey Keithen, Now you have two younger Big brothers!"

"Yes, Yes, I do. So, brothers, do we know how we feel about all of this?" Keithen asked.

"Well, I'm really glad that the truth is finally out. Raynar and Dad both needed to know that they had sons. Dad didn't intend to abandon, run out on Barbara... Raynar didn't mean to run out on Mom... The way I see it, a lack of communication and knowledge is at the root of all of this, however, had things gone down any differently, none of us may be standing here right now! George's determination to Find Keithen's egg, Raynar running to save mom from Grief... Barbara nursing George back to health and George losing his memory, because he would have not ever cheated on Mom... all of it adds up to the three of us standing right here right now.

We are who and how we are because of the 4 of them. We owe them all that we are. Equally..." Braynar explained.

Both of his brothers agreed. The three of them went to talk to the parents to let them know that everything was good in the neighborhood... Thankfully, their parents were at the celebration, already under way on the surface.

Shortly after arriving, all three boys stood up to sing.

They harmonized beautifully together.

AlaHanDrea Rushed over to join them, adding her own whimsical lyrics that had everyone listening, cracking up laughing!

The guys lyrics would pull at the heart strings, while AlaHanDrea's beautiful voice would add whimsical lyrics to lighten the mood...

Athena couldn't resist, she went up and added her beautiful voice to the baby girls... Isabel and Barbara jumped up and joined the girls, adding their awesome voices to the comedic mix, while Raynar and George jumped up and joined the boys...The guys made a tear come to the eye, while the ladies and girls made everyone laugh so hard, they almost peed! The crowd Loved it!

Song after song, the men pulled at the heart, while the ladies kept everyone in stitches!

One big, blended family, having a great time together, reassuring everyone that the crown heads had it all together and were stronger than ever!

Chapters 4

ISABEL AND GEORGE WERE doing their best to adjust to all of the newcomers to Taurus 9.

Although they were always aware of refugees, never before had they had them all up in their faces like the refugees from Ion 6 were!

AlaHanDrea was the reason...

The creatures taking the most adjusting to, were those tiny little elfen fairies.

They flew in swarms and were always tinkering about, fixing things, building things...

Busy little creatures, they were.

They were also some of the baby Queen's best friends and guardians.

Isabel was doing her best to learn patience, but sometimes those helpful tiny creatures could really get on her nerves, but, she tried not to show it, always the gracious queen.

Besides that, they made some incredibly awesome nectar wine! Not as good as the baby Queens nectar wine, but awfully good, just the same.

There were a lot of adjustments to having other creatures on Taurus 9 that shift as well as dragons do...

It was a little hard to get used to, but it was nice... They found themselves socializing with creatures they would have never socialized with before.

But of course, anytime species begin to intermix like that, there are going to be some problems that arise.

But then, there's Good & Bad, Positive/Negative, in everything.

The nightly ground fire gatherings were very pleasant.

Isabel loved how the lions, tigers, bears, Crocs, and others, approached the fires by playing instruments and singing along with the songs in progress...

They'd walk in from every direction, singing and playing...

The Dragons enjoyed the interaction. They had never seen themselves bonding with so many creatures of other species.

Although there was a prophesy about all beasts coming together...

But...

That was just a prophesy...

Wasn't it?

But then, there was the fact that AlaHanDrea's existence seemed to fit in the same prophesy...

The evening air was really pleasant. The drums beginning signaled time to quit for the day.

Time to come hang out with friends, make new friends...

Time to relax and enjoy life for a bit.

A time when all were shifted to neutral, all beasts looked human...

All beast looked the same, as one species...

United...

The tiny fairies didn't grow themselves to everyone else's size average, even though they could have ... Had they really wanted to. They said they looked human enough the size that they were.

It couldn't be argued with... they could communicate...

And, after all, that was the biggest plus to everybody being in human form, as well as wearing the communications collars AlaHanDrea gifted to everyone...open communication between the species.

A dance floor was constructed, then another.

The crowds were growing rather large.

More central fires were built, torches lit...

All of the small bands joined together for 1 large orchestra of musicians and singers.

Merchants made rows to show their wares, concessions stands were erected, portable toilets arrived...

The crowd grew ever larger...

15 couples took one of the stages. They all wore wheeled boots on the their feet!

The second floor quickly filled with couples without wheels...

Yet ..

The music started.

Both dance floors couples began...

Giant viewing screens were behind each dance floor, showing the skater's/dancers large enough to be seen from a far, from the screen...

Both groups showed off their skill.

Then, the second group, comprised of man/dragons & their consorts, placed wheeled boots on their feet, showing off what they had worked so hard to perfect!

Acrobatic dancing with wheels on their feet, just like the refugees!

The competition was really beginning to heat up, when, all of a sudden, a storm began to brew!

Only it wasn't just any storm clouds!

It was a spaceship!

Intruders!

The alarms were sounded all across the land, while creatures of all species, transformed back to natural form and ran for the hills to take cover in order to group together and make a plan!

They were taken completely off guard!

Warriors headed for the hills, all others ran to take cover in the catacombs below the planets surface.

A full scale, planet wide alarm was sounded!

Take cover!

All hands report!

The planet wide council of Kings, summoned AlaHanDrea at once.

"Hello baby girl," George said, welcoming her to the council...

"I suppose you already know about the ship."

"Of course I do," she told them, as she opened a huge viewing screen and began communication attempts...

The Kings looked on while the tiny little girl child, went through communications protocols until finally reaching the intruders...

"Hello, we come from the planet of a nearby star.

My name is JaySon.

Captain JaySon.

This our first attempt at interstellar contact," the creature on the screen said.

Strange looking fella...

"I, am Queen AlaHanDrea.

How can I help you?"

"You?

But, you are a child!

A Baby Child!

Don't you have a grown up I can speak to?"

"You can speak to me and I will decide if you get to speak to anyone else.

We got it that this is your first time to play with your little spaceship, but whoever told you it was okay to barge in on the neighbors, lied to you.

Now, What do you want? You know, You seriously need to back out of our atmosphere! Create an orbit, then contact us and ask permission before you go inserting yourself inside somebody else's atmosphere!

How do you know you don't carry with you, micro organisms that will get off of your ship and contaminate our world?

You don't!

Turn around, leave our atmosphere, place yourself in orbit, and ask permission!

I'll not tell you a second time!

Don't try me!

I might look like a baby, but I can destroy you with very little effort...

Now go!

Do it the right way!

Come in through the front door with permission, or don't come at all!"

The alien ship began to shake... the temperature inside the ship rose!

The hesitant Captain decided, maybe he had better get out of there after all, turned that ship around and went outside the atmosphere, as instructed...

Placed himself in orbit....

Then, tried contacting Taurus 9.

Once again, he reached the baby Queen.

"I did as you instructed.

Please forgive my rudeness and absence of manners... I do apologize and did not realize I was being so rude.

I promise to do better in the future.

Would it be okay now, may I please, speak with an adult?" The alien Captain asked.

"Sure, if that what makes you happy, fine, speak to all the adults you want to speak to.

How about the council of Kings, will that work for you?

Don't bother to answer that, I'll just get them for you."

AlaHanDrea put the counsel of Kings on split screen so everyone could be seen at once, addressing primarily, George, "Your Majesty, King George, this alien is Captain JaySon. He is the creature who so rudely broke up our party. He wishes to speak with grown ups.

Captain JaySon, this is the planetary counsel of Kings. King George is the supreme ruler of the counsel.

Is he grown up enough for you?" AlaHanDrea asked the intruding alien.

"Yes, and, thank you very much, little girl," the alien replied. "Your majesty, greetings. I come to you in peace. This is our first interstellar outreach of exploration. It's very nice to meet you.."

"What is it you want that is so important that you couldn't speak to Queen AlaHanDrea? She is the Alien Ambassador," George asked him

"Pardon my intrusion, your majesty. She is a young child, a little girl and very tiny in size. Why, she couldn't be more than 5, maybe 6 years old, or so."

"She is 6, almost 7. Don't let her size misguide you. She is our alien Ambassador.

Did it occur to you, that on Taurus 9, dealing with primitive civilizations, is considered child's play?" George asked him.

"Primitive? You think us to be Primitive? We are in a starship and you call us primitive?"

"That you think you need a star ship to travel through space is hilarious!

AlaHanDrea, would you mind dealing with this, this, this, primitive?

He is wasting the counsels time and energy.

If you don't feel up to it, we can respect that.

We can always just blow them out of the outer atmosphere, turn them into so much space dust, put them out of our misery..."

"Space dude, why are you bothering us?"AlaHanDrea asked.

"We are out exploring."

"Well, bully for you, y'all learned how to space travel. Tell me, how long did it take you to travel here from your world?"

"27 light years," the Captain replied.

"Ion 6, my home world, was located over 9 billion light years away from here. I traveled here in the course of less than a day.

Yes, you are primitive, very primitive. I can get to your world in a few minutes," she taunted.

"You don't need ships?" He asked.

"You're kidding, right? Why would we do that? First of all, why do we want to go to your world?

But, if we did, we would not rely on ships, how goofy. If you don't have travel tunnels, you are so far behind!

Most inhabited planets with intelligent beings, travel through tunnels, geeeesh, not very bright, are you?

Go home JaySon, go home, grow up and quit bothering the neighbors.

Didn't anybody ever tell you, that just because you can do something, doesn't always mean that you should?" She taunted.

"You're not being very nice."

"Exactly. We don't like you and don't want you here. You have a planet of your own, go stay on it." She replied.

"Are you not curious about life on other planets?" He asked.

"You are not very bright at all.

We already know there is life on other planets.

It's stupid to think there isn't.

We just believe in leaving them alone and minding our own business. We don't go sticking our noses into others business.

We don't wish to trade with you, or even have contact with you.

Just go home.

I will save you time and energy. More planets than you can count, are inhabited.

None of which, wants you bothering them!

Stay home and quit spreading your germs all over the galaxy!

Compared to most life forms, you are extremely primitive.

Go home, grow up and learn a valuable lesson... stay on your own planet!

You have enough problems to deal with, to be out trying to add more to the list.

Try spending your effort, your time, your money, fixing your planets relations between your people... stuff like that... Go cure diseases, stop wars, end hunger and leave the rest of us alone... Go home, JaySon."

"Before I leave, I have crew members that don't want to return, because of the length of time it takes us to return.

Would it be okay if some of our crew where to come to the ground level, I mean, to the surface of your planet... possibly stay?"

"You have refugees?" She asked.

"Yes, they are begging to stay. We have all been traveling a very long time and they insist that they will not survive if I make them stay aboard for the trip back.

They had no idea what they were in for... none of us really did, because, none of us have ever journeyed this far before. They say they just can't take being in the ship another day, much less 27 more light years."

"Bring the refugees to the viewing screen."

The alien Captain did as instructed. George took one look at them and approved their request to land. Jax appeared with a transport tunnel and the refugees were loaded up into the tunnel.

They were in absolute awe of all that they saw. Some were released on Taurus 9 and placed into quarantine. The rest were taken home.

Before they knew it, they were exiting the tunnel back on their own planet. Jax requested a local newspaper, which, was retrieved rather quickly, then Jax closed the tunnel and returned to the ship.

Once he arrived, he handed the newspaper to the captain, told him that his crew members were already back home and told him to go join them.

"You mean, you've already been to my planet and returned?" The captain asked.

"I mean just that. Now, go home!"

Another group of weary travelers rushed the deck, begging to be transported home. Mr Jax loaded them into the tunnel and took part of the second group to Taurus 9 for quarantine and the rest of the second group were taken home. Jax loaded one of the first passengers back up, and returned her to the ship.

She explained to the captain how short a trip it really was, once you knew how to properly travel.

Mr. Jax took the woman and returned to the surface.

He went into chamber with George.

A few minutes later, Jax and a small group of royal guard, boarded the alien ship, examining crew members, then transported them to Taurus 9, placing them into quarantine.

Approximately 40 crew members were taken to the surface.

Captain JaySon decided he had enough of trying to be peaceful and it was time to teach these neighbors a lesson in manners!

They might be primitive in travel, but they had great weapons!

When the dragons attempted to attack the ship, they discovered the alien ship had weapons that blocked the magic of the dragons!

AlaHanDrea was furious!

She threw shields up to protect the dragons!

She watched while a squadron of fighters flew out of the big ship!

The dragons were no match for the squadron of fighters!

AlaHanDrea ordered the dragons to retreat! Then, she put out a distress call to the elfen fairies!

Tens of thousands of the tiny fairies took to the skies, led by their queen!

The dragons sat and watched while the tiny little elfen fairies engaged in battle against the invading aliens!

They were in total disbelief of what they were seeing!

They couldn't believe their eyes!

Those tiny little creatures were making short work of the alien ships!

The ships couldn't see the tiny creatures!

They were helpless against the fairies and the fairies magic!

It didn't take very long at all before the fighter ships began falling to the ground and exploding or flying off, out of control, into the vastness of space!

The fairies focussed on the main ship, infiltrated it and began destroying every thing inside... Control panels, engine rooms, weapons bays...

Anyone that got in their way, quickly discovered that fairies had fangs with fast working, deadly venom, as well as being able to spin webs and cocoon creatures at lightening speeds!

They were too small and too fast! In the course of a few short minutes, all crew members of the big ship were dead, or cocooned, except for the captain...

He stood inside of a protection chamber, paralyzed in fear, with swarms of fairies staring at him, ready to end him! Their venom worked in seconds.

The dragons had no idea that fairies were such deadly creatures!

AlaHanDrea decided to transport the captain to the planets surface, along with the cocooned crew, then exploded the alien ship and it's weapons along with it.

All of the aliens were quarantined.

The elfen fairies suffered zero casualties!

The counsel of Kings were duly impressed!

They had no idea those tiny creatures were such vicious warriors!

They discovered that size really doesn't matter after all!

6" could be quite effective......

Chapter 4

The alien Captain was relieved when his cocoon was finally opened.

However, he remained in a cage. Still, it wasn't that cocoon!

The cage wasn't really so bad, at least it was spacious and comfortable.

"Your majesty, it's time to unwrap the quarantined aliens," Craigen told his king.

"Thank you Craigen. Say, Jax, how do you think we should handle this situation?" George asked.

"George, I'm not sure they even know who they are. You might try shifting in front of them and see what their reactions are. But, I don't believe that we are wrong."

"Ya, neither do I. Ok, it's a worth a try." George agreed, then went to the aliens and shifted right in front of them!

The stunned silence was finally broken by one of the females. "Are you not afraid of being caught?" she asked.

"Caught? Who is to Catch me? Dragons Rule this World!" George told her.

The stunned look on all of their faces were priceless.

George asked them, "Why do you fear being caught? Who would catch you, you are a Dragon!"

"Dragons are executed when discovered! Shifting is illegal!" she replied.

"Not in this world, it isn't! Dragons RULE this world!" George growled.

"Seriously? Dragons Rule the planet?" she asked, in disbelief.

"You were taken from that ship because we recognized you as one of us. I have someone I want you to meet. Mr. Jax here is a Watcher. It's his job, as well as other watchers, to relocate deserving species when a planet is about to die.

Dragons were evacuated from our home and brought to the Milky Way Galaxy. We were all supposed to be brought to Taurus 9, but a glitch in communication, caused our kind to be dispersed to several planets, not just Taurus 9.

I strongly suspect that you are part of the lost tribes. Can you shift?" George asked her.

"You mean, right here? In front of others? Oh, I dare not! I will be killed! I cannot risk anyone to find out!" she quietly cried.

"No one is going to hurt you here. If you're worried about returning to your world, don't, because you're not! You are here to stay! You are finally home, right where you belong!" Jax told the frightened girl.

She attempted to shift, but only partially shifted, then returned to human state. "I can't! Oh, I just cannot!" She cried, shaking in fear!

The other Aliens in her same cage gathered around, "Is it true? Dragons rule this world?" a young man asked.

"Yes, we do!" George answered, then was interrupted...

"Your majesty, I don't mean to disturb you, but, we have a bit of a situation. Do I have your permission to eat Captain JaySon?" Thomlin asked his king.

"I take it he is being a problem? Have the Fairies help escort the good Captain over here first, please. I'd like for him to answer a few questions first, then, you can eat him, or feed him to these fine dragons!" George replied.

"I thought they looked familiar! As you wish, your majesty."

"Good guy, that Thomlin!"

"Your majesty?" the girl asked.

"Yes, I am the supreme king, Ruler of Taurus 9!" George exclaimed, then shifted and let out a ground shaking roar!

Chapter 5

The refugees were rapidly growing in numbers, as watchers combed the Milky Way, looking for misplaced Flock.

The watcher king saw the errors in relocating dragon kind, as a black eye on the entire race!

It would take a while for the proud king to calm down over the situations...

The new society of dragons, were having a difficult time adjusting, so, a law was imposed.

All new arrivals, were required to remain in dragon state, or, their natural state, 24/7, until cleared to shift.. in hopes that living as their true selves, would help them to regain their natural selves.

Feeding time was interesting.

The alien dragons cooked food like humans did!

Being sophisticated dragons, the Taurus 9 flocks, were willing to give just about anything a try, to include, eating food cooked in pans, on a stove, or, over a fire.

The newbe's loved all of the shape shifting creatures and the fact that they, too, were recent refugees.

The attention they received had mixed reactions. Attention is nice, but just like with water, too much will drown a fella.

For way too long, creatures were forced to hide who they really were... disguising themselves as their enemy, in order to survive.

For the first time in centuries, the newcomers were free to just be themselves...

In their natural states.

As dragons, they were clumsy, at best!

None of them had been to their pubescent classes with a love dragon, such as the Taurus 9 love dragon, Lord Pooky.

They had received no training whatsoever in the arts of physical pleasure and/or romance!

There were no experts in the art of training and preparing Virgins...

There were no nightly ground fires and socializing on their old planet.

Young dragons didn't have the benefit of a flock to teach and guild them...

Their ability to do magic with stifled, to say the least.

It was akin to having to learn to walk all over again.

The newcomers did not even remember how to speak to each other telepathically.

Raising infants was easier than trying to train grown ass dragons!

Way easier!

The search for other lost tribes continued...

KING GEORGE AND THE counsel of Kings, called a planet wide address... Beyond huge Viewing screens popped up all across Drakonia.

Dragons gathered in their communities to create watch parties, in order to listen to what their leaders had to say to them.

"Greetings Flocks, thank you for your attention this day.

It does our hearts good to have our lost tribes returning to us!

Hopefully, the days of suffering for dragon kind, throughout the galaxy, are coming to an end!"

Cheers rose up from all corners of the globe!

"Today, I would like to speak to y'all, concerning one of the most valuable members of our combined communities, Queen AlaHanDrea, aka The Baby Queen.

For those of you that have not yet had the pleasure of meeting her, she came to us from Ion 6, at the tender age of 6 years old, as an orphan, with a tremendous support system, made up of a wide variety of creatures, that she happens to share DNA with.

As an infant, as well as a little girl, a 6-in high, six year old, little girl, she is more powerful than any creature we have ever witnessed.

We are fortunate, in that, we have had the pleasure of getting to know her from very early in her life. We have the privilege of being a part of her growing years, her developing years, her childhood...

We have the privilege of being a part of her life, the very creatures that help her learn and grow into an adult.

We, are becoming a part of her history, as well as her future!

Ours is a blessed gift, the gift of being a part of her world And her life.

There is an amazing amount of responsibility that comes with this gift that we have been given.

The Baby Queen came to Taurus 9 as an orphaned child.

Therefore, raising her correctly is the responsibility of her community!

It is up to all of us to insure that she is always treated with the utmost respect!

Is up to all of us to ensure that no one takes advantage of her emotionally.

I have no fear of anyone being able to hurt her physically...

Her emotional well being is in all of our hands.

Once she begins reaching her transitional age, it is the responsibility of each and every one of us to make certain no one takes advantage of her weakened state due to raging hormones!

We owe it to her to help her reach her adult hood, pure!

It is easy to see that she will be an absolute beauty as a woman, just look at her as a small child!

She is gorgeous now! Heads turn when she walks by.

No matter the species, her beauty is appreciated.

Her beauty is not restricted to the physical ... She is beautiful through and through.

As a woman, she will be irresistible, but I say to you!

Resist!

Until which time she reaches her full adulthood...

Resist!

Queen AlaHanDrea is OUR baby...

Our Child...

She is the child of Taurus 9 and collectively, let's raise a balanced and well adjusted adult!

An adult without the emotional scarring that so many suffer from!

Love Her, Protect Her, respect And appreciate her! Most of all, cherish her!

To Queen AlaHanDrea! SALUTE!"

The crowd yelled, "TO QUEEN ALAHANDREA, SALUTE!"

The screen went quiet for a moment, when it came back on, baby girl was on it. The crowd went wild with cheers!

She threw her fist in the air and hollered, "Queen ALAHANDREA!"

The cheers were deafening!

Then, she looked at the screen in such a way it was as if she was staring everyone straight in their eyes and talking directly to them as an individual, " please know, that I love and appreciate each and every one of you!

All y'all are my family... all of you... each and every one of you... are very important to me. Together... all of us together... are Taurus 9!

When aliens attack us, they attack all of us!

We are all the children of Taurus 9!

Love and respect each other every bit as much as you love and respect me! Together we are 1! Together, we are strong!

Together we are unstOPPABLE!" She blew kisses and the crowd, again, went wild!

The dark screen was only visible for a few more seconds, before vanishing as quickly as it had appeared.

THE HUMAN SECTORS WEREN'T real sure how they felt about all the new comers.

They weren't certain how they felt about the broadcast they had over heard.....

The broadcast made them more determined than ever to try to replicate the process that created the baby girls parents, then her...

They wanted to possess as well as control a creature of her magnitude!

The Science community was under the misguided illusion that creating a creature, meant they would have control over it!

As if ..!

They had a whole lot to learn!

Chapter 6

Leon, Dane and AlaHanDrea were spending quite a bit of time together, exploring, playing like good children play... Tommy was often with them as well.

The four of them were pretty much inseparable.

The baby girl had cocooned Tommy and made a few changes in him, physically, to even his playing field, as AlaHanDrea liked to put it.

Tommy was far from still being the frail, timid little fella the kids had first met!

He loved his new life!

He also loved all three of his friends very much...

Leon and Dane were his Heros!

Life with the pack was far from his life as a human...

A few other shifting creature children, also hung out with the kids on most days, but those four were the core group.

Tommy felt like a prince, because, he was treated like a prince... It didn't go to his head, tho. He was still Tommy in every way that mattered.

As strange as it may sound, he was more comfortable living with the creatures.

ALAHANDREA'S 8TH BIRTHDAY party celebration had been quite spectacular!

So much so, that she insisted her birthday celebrations be about all children, not just her.

She wanted her birthday to be a time to celebrate children in general.

King George and the counsel, agreed, making her birthday an official holiday to celebrate all children!

3 days were set aside and the celebrations became akin to a state fair...

When her 9th birthday came, she assumed that Dane would be joining her, as usual, but that morning came and only Tommy showed up.

Danes visits had slowed way down in recent months, but she thought for sure he'd be there for her birthday! Especially her last birthday as a single digit!

AlaHanDrea called for Athena at once, worried that something bad had happened to her Dane.

Tommy tried not to be offended.

"Sweet girl, mer boys grow up at a different rate than most other males you encounter.

He is now 11 years old.

Officially, he is now a merman.

He is no longer a boy.

As a merman, as well as a crown prince, he now has responsibilities.

He's also got raging hormones ..

He has become interested in females in ways that you are much too young for!

Baby girl, he still loves his baby Queen and nothing will ever change that! But for now, Dane is finding himself, exploring what it means to be growing into a man... " She explained.

"Oh, he's wanting to have sex and make baby Danes..." She said, sarcastically...

"Well, ya, pretty much," she agreed.

"Ya, he can't do that with me. I'm no longer a baby, but I'm not a woman either and I'm not doing that!

But, Athena, does that mean that he won't be coming to..." She was interrupted...

"There's my pretty little queen!" Dane said as he walked up, fist filled with cut flowers.

"Dane!" She squealed! Then put the flowers in a vase. " Thank you , Dane, they are lovely!" She told him, smiling really big at him.

"Athena, if you and Tommy will excuse us for a moment, I need to see my girl alone," Dane told them, as he took AlaHanDrea's hand and led her over by the water falls, where they could have some privacy.

"I have a few things for you, for your birthday and because I love you so much!" He told her, handing her box number 1.

"Oh Dane, you shouldn't have! But, since you did," she teased as she tore the paper off and looked inside the box.

A beautiful heavy gold chain was inside of the most gorgeous hand carved box. Dane fastened the chain around her neck for her.

The second box contained earrings. He helped her slip them on... Staring into her beautiful eyes...

They got lost in a gaze for a moment, then he leaned down and kissed her softly on the lips, then kissed her a little longer on the lips...

A regular kiss, but AlaHanDrea knew what Athena was trying to tell her...

Then, he produced a small little bitty box.

When she opened it, a beautiful ring was inside!

Dane took it out, placed it on her finger and kissed her again.

"I love you, AlahanDrea. I know that you love me, too.

These pieces of jewelry are my promise to you that I'm now and always have been, your Dane.

Baby girl, that's not about to change.

There's something that I need to talk to you about.

You see, there's this girl that I want to see.

I'm growing up, very quickly, too. I have certain needs.... This girl is a mer and she will let me do things that, well, you need to be a whole lot older to do, according to my sister.

One of these days, you and I will explore these things together, but until then, I need to explore, experiment, learn and grow.

I may even fall in love, but baby girl, no one ever comes before you!

You are my life love!

These will be my growing up loves...

No one will ever compare to you!

You own my heart, girl!"

He took her in his arms and hugged her close.

They held that embrace, enjoying the emotions running between them.

"Oh, but that you were only old enough now, today now... Girl, girl, girl..."

She knew Dane was Right. She also knew he had to be free to grow up ... She already felt a growing in his pants when he hugged her!

"Yes, Dane, I do love you!

I always will!

And yes, my young love, I am far too young!

Can you bring her and still come play with us?

Are you too old to still play?"

"I'll see what I can do", he smiled that gorgeous smile of his and kissed her again.

AlaHanDrea loved her jewelry, the kissing thing, she had mixed feelings about ..

She'd wait for Dane, wait for herself to grow up...

Once she was a woman... then, he could focus on her and maybe quit the other girls!

Maybe then, she would enjoy the whole kissing thing a bit more...

Tommy was patiently waiting for her return and was enjoying his rare time alone with Athena. Her beauty was mesmerizing!

Even young men had a difficult time resisting her!

Tommy was older than Dane by 2 years or so, and was already in the throws of puberty..

His voice was changing, etc...

AlaHanDrea tried to ignore the changes in her Tommy. She wasn't ready for her 3 best friends to become men yet...

Leon actually beat Dane in reaching manhood... But then,.Leon was a feline. They are ready at a year old!

DANE HAD HAD HIS EYE on Kareena for a long time.

She was an incredibly beautiful mermaid.

He didn't think she had noticed him!

But, she noticed, alright! Who wouldn't notice a handsome prince, future King!?

The two of them went for a swim, played around a sunken ship for a bit, then Kareena enticed Dane to follow her up to the surface, a little far away. She knew of a place where the two of them could be alone together, without being seen.

He eagerly followed her up, shifting to drylander right away.

They used their magic to create a bit of a nest.

Once they had their new area set up, Kareena stood in front of Dane and dropped her dress!

She had no other clothing on!

She stood before Dane completely nude!

He stood there, stunned, admiring her youthful beauty , grinning ear to ear.

Kareena slowly removed his shirt for him, then slid his trousers down, touching him in ways he'd never been touched!

The two young lovers had no problem figuring things out!

Dane had no idea how incredible it felt before that moment!

As wonderful as finishing felt, he wanted more! They explored each other, time and time again!

A couple of times they thought they heard something, but quickly dismissed it, going right back at what they were doing.

Time actually got away from them and before they knew it, the sun was beginning to set!

They both jumped up, left their clothes and jumped back into the sea, heading for home!

No mer was supposed to be out swimming at night so far away from the community!

The world was far too dangerous of a place!

Dane had Kareena by the hand, pulling her along, swimming just as fast as he could!

Kareena screamed and he sped up without looking!

He just swam for all he was worth, hanging tightly onto Kareena's hand, determined to get them both safely home.

Kareena started to scream again, but stopped.

Dane sped up even more!

He thought he felt something, his fin was stinging, so he continued to hold her hand as tightly as he could and swam for all he was worth!

Suddenly, he found himself surrounded by royal guard!

Completely surrounded!

One of the guards pried Kareena hand from Danes, while another guard kept Dane looking at him, as he pulled Dane into a chamber of his father's cave.

The guard made Dane lay down, which, Dane Didn't want to do, but, the guard insisted.

"Prince Dane, your highness, whose hand were you holding when we found you?"

"What do you mean?

You know who Kareena is!" He answered, feeling confused.

"Oh, o.k. that was miss Kareena, thank you, your highness, we will inform her parents at once."

"What do you mean, was Miss Kareena? You'll inform her parents? Where is Kareena? I need to see her!" He hollered, in a panic.

King Neptune came rushing in, as did Athena.

Both were in a state of near panic!

The sound of voices arguing with the guards had Neptune going out to deal with the upset, instructing Athena to stay with her baby brother...

"Athena, what's going on? Why was I told to remain laying down and where is Kareena? Why were guards all over me? " He asked.

"Little bother, Kareena is dead. What's more, her father thinks You did it!"

"What?!?!" Dane screamed!

"Dane, Kareena is dead, did you not know? You had her hand in yours!" Athena was unsure how Dane couldn't have known!

"Sure I had her hand, I was pulling her, because I swim so much faster than her!

Where is she?" Dane cried.

"Well, she's in many places, little brother when the guards found you, all you had of her was her arm!" Athena told him.

NO! NO NO NO NO NO NO NO NO!" Dane screamed!

AlaHanDrea froze in mid motion. Tommy stopped, "AlaHanDrea, what's wrong? What's happening?" Tommy asked.

"It's Dane!

Something's terribly wrong!

I heard him screaming! Athena just told me to stay put and to stay out of it!" She told Tommy.

"Then stay put and stay out of it," Tommy echoed.

A moment later, bubbling in the nearby pool announced the arrival of Mers.

It was King Neptune!

AlaHanDrea got a bad feeling deep in her gut!

"King Neptune, what is it? What's wrong with Dane?"

She asked, the worry obvious in her voice.

"Baby girl, something terrible has happened. I'm not sure quite how to say this, cuz I know Dane loves you, but he was with another girl, and now that girl is dead."

"What? Oh, I knew he was going to see another girl, he already told me that before he did it, he's a good young man, your majesty, but how is she dead? What happened?"

"That's what we all want to know. When the guards found him, he was swimming, holding her hand and arm and the rest of her was missing. The guards found pieces of her scattered across the floor of the sea. When they gathered up the pieces, they discovered more than one girls pieces.

Several young girls bodies were torn to pieces laying on the bottom of the sea.

Not all mers.

There are those that think Dane did it!

My son would not do something like that!

We need your help baby girl ... we need your help to find out what happened to those girls and to clear my son before something terrible happens!

Please!

I beg of you!

Help us now!

Your Dane needs you!

Athena needs you!

I need you!

Dane is my boy, my son, my heir, my heart. Please, AlaHanDrea, please help us find the truth and clear my boy," the distraught king cried.

Chapter 7

AlaHanDrea was determined to find out what was going on with those murders.

She was beside herself! She couldn't understand how anybody could possibly think that Dane was capable of anything as horrible as killing another, much less mangling them!

The distraught young Queen called her fairies together, enlisting their help to investigate the situation.

When they met for the first time after the investigation began, the fairies told her that they had seen something unusual in an area near where Dane and his girlfriend had made a nest.

The fairies were sure it was Danes spot, because they had left their clothing behind.

The fairies also told her that they didn't investigate any closer, because their senses told them there was something very dangerous there... something very scary, dangerous there ... and that she should proceed with extreme caution... even though she was a very powerful creature, they feared that this, whatever it was, could hurt her.

When Alahandrea's reached the nest Dane and his girl had made, it made her feel very uneasy, seeing their clothes on the ground, knowing what they had done together.

Then, she saw it! There was a trail that looked as if something had scooted across the ground from behind some close by bushes....

Danalli, Keithen and Braynar were visiting their favorite island.

The food wagon was delivered shortly after their arrival.

Danalli had a practice of asking food why it was food... What they had done to earn them a spot in the food wagon.

Danalli was fascinated by the sins people committed that they deemed worthy of death by dragons.

Much to his surprise, a beautiful young woman was in the wagon.

He took her out of the cage to question her, unlike the other food, whom he questioned while still in the cage.

"What, pray tell, has you on my menu today, you don't stink of sin!"

The terrified young woman could barely speak, trembling with fear.

Danalli was not without compassion. He shackled her, then shifted to man state right in front of her!

"There, now, am I less terrifying now?"

"Ya ya ya yes," she stammered.

"Hi, I'm Prince Danalli, heir to the throne of Drakonia. One of three heirs, actually. Ya know, we usually only eat sinners, you don't stink of sin, so, please, tell me about you."

"Ma ma ma ma my na na na na name is Gail. My husband put me in the food wagon to take his place. I said nothing to the wagon master, because I'd rather be eaten by a dragon than to have that horrible man touch me!

My father sold me to him, but I am sickened by the sight of him!"

"It's very nice to meet you, Gail. If you will excuse me a moment, I am kind of hungry and I don't want my brothers to eat all of the food. I won't be gone long, I will go ahead and eat fast this time!" He said as he left her side.

Screams from their meals had Gail hiding her face and covering her ears, as she laid on the ground, crying in terror.

A short time later, Danalli was picking her up off of the ground, gently brushing her off, then used his magic to produce a comfortable lounge to sit on.

"I'm not going to eat you, Gail. Well, not in the sense of filling my belly," he said, with a naughty wink.

"I didn't know dragons are men, too."

"Most humans don't. It's our way of protecting ourselves."

"If you don't mind my saying so, Prince Danalli, you're a very handsome man, as a human. Very handsome. You're so big and strong!"

"Well, I'm a dragon! We tend to be rather large and muscular," he teased.

"Anyway, why would I choose to shift into an ugly human?" He teased

"How long can you stay as a human?"

"For as long as I choose."

"What are you going to do with me, if you're not going to eat me?"

"I'm going to keep you, as my pet.

You were given to me, you belong to me, you are mine. I choose to not eat you today.

No, I will not let you go. Should you attempt to escape, I will kill you without hesitation.

It's impossible to hide from me, I know your smell and it cannot be disguised.

My sense of smell is far too good for that.

You are very beautiful, Gail. I will enjoy keeping you as my pet. Worry not, we are good to our pets, we love our pets..."

"Danalli, bro, are you playing with your food again" Keithen asked him through the door.

"Haha, funny man.

Ya, I am, actually. Thought I'd keep this one."

"O.k., well, what ever you're doing, do it kind of quickly. Baby girl needs us to return home. There's something going on back there..."

"O.k. give me just a minute..."

"Well, it looks like we are going to have to go sooner than I had expected.

You will ride on my back for the trip home, but for now..."

Danalli stood up, then unshackled her.

When he raised back up, he took her by the shoulders, looked deep into her eyes, then kissed her the sweetest kiss!

It took her by surprise and she didn't know how to react!

Then he gazed into her eyes again, then kissed her with a bit more passion, this time, she melted in his arms!

That was the reaction he was looking for!

He knew in that moment, that she'd make a fine pet!

He stroked her hair while gazing into her eyes again... "I could really love you, Gail. Yes, I sure could!" He kissed her again, this time, allowing his hands to find some of her places and making her squirm under his touch ..

"Bro! C'mon, baby girl needs us! There have been some murders back home!" Braynar called out

Danalli stopped what he was doing, "Murders? What? O.k. brothers, be right there " he answered

"sorry about that. We can finish this after we find out what's going on back home.

One of our Queens needs our help.

Just do what I say do, and no one will hurt you."

Danalli took her outside, shifted and Braynar placed her on Danalli's back, strapping her into a harness. "O.K. bro, she's all strapped in, let's go!" Braynar told him, then shifted back to dragon state.

"Hold on tight! But don't worry, you won't fall off.." Braynar told the frightened woman.

Gail had not ever flown before, especially not on the back of a dragon!

The harness was comfortable enough, she felt pretty secure, actually.

The view was breathtaking!

It was a little rough while Danalli was flapping his wings, but once he had gained altitude and began to soar, the flight was really nice!

Her thoughts were on those kisses and his knowledge of the female body.... As well as the fact that he told her that he could really love her... she had never been touched the way Danalli touched her, or held the way he held her... And never was she kissed like Danalli kissed her!

She held her arms out to the side, tilted her head back and relished the feel of the wind! It felt as if she, herself were flying!

Danalli felt the change in her and asked Braynar telepathically for a report... "she's falling in love with you, bro!"

Danalli just smiled!

The scared young woman was beginning to feel as tho she were reborn into a fantasy world of splendor!

She began singing.

She didn't think anyone could hear her from up there.

By the second verse, Danalli began singing with her!

She was shocked! But loved it at the same time. They sang together quite nicely. Their voices blended well together.

The singing seemed to really calm her! Much to her own surprise, she felt happy that she climbed into that food wagon!

The trip was a rather lengthy one, the singing really helped to pass the time.

Gail loved Danalli's deep, bass voice. She knew that she could listen to him sing and never grow tired of hearing it.

Before they landed, and much to her own surprise, she had fallen in love with Danalli, both as a man and as a dragon!

She was thinking how she'd love to be more to him than just a pet... He stole her heart away!

Landing was almost sad. She was really enjoying soaring through the heavens on the back of a mighty dragon! Who'd of ever thought she'd be doing that?

Once on the ground, Danalli took her into his cave.

She was surprised to see his cave.

It was much more modern than anything she'd have guessed!

Not at all what she expected!

He put her in her cage and locked the door. Then, he opened the door, took her in his arms and kissed her the kind of kiss that made her melt in his arms! Then, closed and locked the cage doors again.

"I won't be any longer than I have to be. I promise. Should anything happen to prevent my return for any reason, Braynar or Keithen will be here for you. Try not to worry.

While I'm gone, feel free to fix up your cage.

You'll find that you have many rooms.

A couple of the rooms have crates full of stuff. Look through them and use any of it that you find that you like.

Most of it is salvage things from shipwrecks and that sort of thing... just stuff that I've collected that I found interesting.

Make yourself comfortable and make this space your own.

Don't worry, no one will dare to hurt you!

You belong to me!

Now, Come here and kiss me goodby," he instructed her.

She went over to the barred wall of her cage and kissed him through the bars.

Once he was gone, she turned on the stereo and began exploring her huge cage.

He was right, there were many rooms!

And a ton of stuff!

Most of it was obviously from a ship or 3.

Danalli joined Keithen and Braynar for a meeting. They were being briefed by the tiny fairies.

ALAHANDREA FOLLOWED the scoot marks to the waters edge.

What ever it was, entered the water... From the looks of things, whatever it was, followed Dane...

She was following it's trail, which implied it didn't float.

It scooted across the floor of the sea.

When she first saw it, she wasn't sure what she was seeing.

It took a moment for her to realize she was looking at a creature!

It was ugly!

She had not ever seen anything like it before in her life!

It was a huge, blobby thing with eyes all over it and way too many arms! Each arm had a mouth at the end of it that was full of long, sharp teeth! One big central mouth was on the body part, with eyes all around... It was a hideous looking creature!

Alahandrea threw a forcefield up around it to imprison it and headed back to the surface to get her dragons to come have a look.

As soon as she was gone, the creature dissolved the forcefield and began scooting along the bottom of the sea until it reached a cavern. He entered it and began scooting along, exploring...

Gail thought she heard something, then decided it was her imagination and went back to unpacking crates.

When she carried a few things to the main front room of her cage, she found 2 huge bushels of fruit with a note from Danalli.

She figured that what she had heard was the fruit arriving, then went back to going through the trunks of stuff... decorating her area.

It was beginning to look like a home!

She even found some rugs for the floor!

The sound of something dragging or scooting got her attention.

This time, she knew she heard something!

Fear gripped her as she slowly got up to go see what it was..

She screamed in terror when she saw that horrible blobby thing creature scooting towards her cage!

She reached for some fruit and threw the fruit through the bars. The blobby thing quickly gobbled it up. So, she threw another banana and it quickly ate it.

"Oh, you like that, huh? Want another nanner? Huh? Nanner nanner?" She asked it

"Nanner Nanner" it said!

"Oh, you can speak! Here, here's a nanner for you," and she threw another.

"Nanner, Nanner" it said....

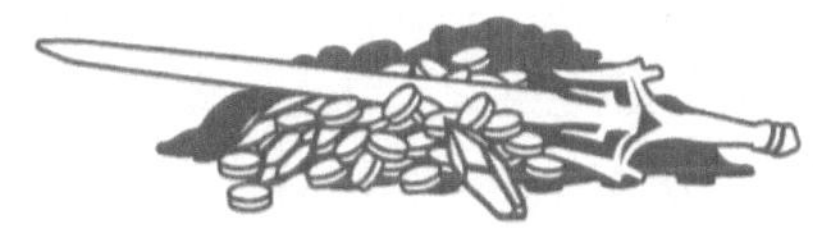

ALAHANDREA RAN INTO the fairies camp, where the guys were.

She told them what she had found and what she had done to hold it.

The sound of someone screaming rang out!

The men all looked at each other and hollered Gail! At the same time!

Gail had run out of bananas and was throwing other kinds of fruit. "Want an apple? Apple? She asked

"Apple, nanner Nanner apple." It said.

"My name is Gail," she said, patting her chest.

"Gail, nanner Nanner, apple, Gail." It said, slowly scooting closer.

"Do you have a name?"

"Gail, nanner Nanner apple Gail,"

"O.k. well, I'm going to call you Bob. Bob."

"Bob Gail Nanner Nanner Bob apple Gail Bob Gail."

Gail threw kiwi fruits. "Kiwi kiwi."

Bob picked up the kiwi then threw it down "fffffwwwu kiwi, Bob kiwi fffffwu"

"O.k. well no kiwi"

"No kiwi, ffffwu, kiwi. Fffffwwwu." His arms were flailing about.

"O.k. Bob, no more Kiwi. Orange, Orange," Gail said, trying desperately to figure out a way out of the terrifying situation.

Bob picked up the orange and shoved it into his mouth. "O-range o-range, Gail nanner Nanner apple orange Gail," Bob said.

The creature finally got close to the bars and made the cage walls disappear!

There was nothing between it and her!

It began to scoot towards Gail, saying "Nanner Nanner, apple, o-range Gail....." Arms flailing ever which way...

Suddenly, AlaHanDrea appeared.

Bob slapped her, sending her flying into the wall!

Gail screamed, so, Bob screamed!

AlahanDrea froze Bob.

"Don't be afraid, I'm queen AlaHanDrea, I'm here to help you," she told the terrified young lady.

"Queen Ala han Drea, nanner nanner Apple O-range o-range Gail nanner nanner Bob Gail Bob Gail."

"It speaks!" Alahandrea exclaimed. Before it could totally break free, the baby queen made a huge viewing screen appear and made Bob's memories play across the screen.

What she saw made her furious!

He was created in a laboratory by human scientists! In an attempt to recreate a creature like her!

Oh! she was furious!

This time the baby Queen put a force field around Gail, then put a second field around Gail, then used her magic to replace the bars, making them twice as thick, then vanished.

She was only gone for a moment before returning. She had placed a feeding cage just outside of the cave.

The cage contain the scientists that created Bob, then released him in Drakonia, along with other failures!

Danalli and his brothers appeared a moment after their young Queen returned.

They were stunned by what they saw.

Bob broke Free so AlaHanDrea showed him where the caged scientist were and he began to scoot.

She told the guys not to move ... don't move a muscle... let him pass.

Bob scooted ever so slowly, arms flailing about toward the scientist cage.

He kept saying bad bad kiwi kiwi bad bad kiwi bad bad kiwi kiwi bad bad man kiwi Bad man kiwi" as he scooted ever closer.. the scientist saw him coming toward them and began screaming in terror.

Danalli rushed over to Gail.

AlaHanDrea removed the forcefield..

Screams rang out as Bob reached through the bars of the cage and pulled out each scientist through the bars, tearing them to pieces as he pulled them out.

What he did to the bodies was absolutely gross.

It was obvious to everyone who committed the murders.

It was Bob!

They didn't blame Bob though, they blamed the scientists that they fed to Bob.

Bob stood outside looking at the mess he made and began to cry!

That big blobby thing began to boohoo with tears running out of every one of his eyes.

It didn't look so scary when it was crying.

The crying accelerated to wah haahaa and boohoo, over and over with tears just pouring.

It's hard to be angry at a creature that's crying so hard.

Obvious sorrow like that makes you want to comfort the creature, but no one dared get near Bob, he was too terrifying!

He had way too many mouths with way too many sharp teeth.

But it was obvious the poor thing was in emotional pain.

Then all of a sudden, Bob began to convulse & stretch out in all kinds of weird directions... for a moment there, it looked like he would explode! Then, much to everyone's shock, Bob turned into a man! "Nanner nanner," he said, sniffling.

Danalli used his magic to clothe the man.

"Well Bob, look at you!" Gail said.

"Bob" was all he said.

Alahandrea immediately threw up viewing screens all under the sea, especially in Neptune's home. She also sent screens for Mr Jax and Raynar to see...

Video footage of Bob's memories began to play, from his creation until that day.

The footage was very difficult to watch in places, especially the parts showing the murders...

Her Dane was vindicated!

But now, what to do about Bob?

The creature didn't realize he was murdering the girls.

He was hungry.

He didn't know any better, he hadn't been taught anything, just dumped out in Drakonia.

He could speak and shift, so, was it right to execute him?

He was a one of kind creature of great power, not unlike baby girl, in that aspect.

A counsel met immediately to decide his fate.

The royal brothers shifted to go join the meeting. Bob watched them, then shifted to dragon state!

Everyone stood, staring, in total disbelief!

"Well, shoot, Bob, you may as well join us, then! Come on, follow us and Bob, don't be killing anyone or Anything unless one of us tells you too! Got it?"

"Bob"

"O.K. well, keep up and let's go," Braynar told him.

The young queen joined the meeting by video screen, she wanted to stay with Gail.

They discovered that Bob had started crying because he was excited to see the scientist that created him and attempted to hug them. He hadn't meant to destroy them!

The same was true for the girls!

Truth be known, he preferred to eat vegetation and fruit.

He saw them and was lonely. He hadn't meant to kill them. He wasn't very good with his arms that had mouths for hands and teeth as fingers.

He was scared and alone, not understanding why he was dumped out in the wilderness, all by himself.

After killing who he deemed as his parents, he shifted to man state in hopes of not mangling anyone else.

He hadn't intended to Kill Gail. He loved her as much as bananas. That's what he had been trying to say!

He wanted and needed a hug! He was lonely and scared!

Looking like a dragon earned him compassion.

Once he figured out that he could shift, he found that he could shift to look like anything he wanted to look like!

It was finally decided that the dragons would be responsible for Bob.

They would teach him and train him and help him to be a productive member of their society, minus killing anyone.

The only thing that really bothered them about Bob, was the fact that he was extremely powerful. Not quite as powerful as the baby girl, but was close to being as powerful as her, which was, in itself, pretty scary...

Chapter 8

King Neptune was beside himself after seeing that Dane had a big bite taken out of his fin.

The whole ordeal had Dane in a state of shock and grief.

It barely registered to him that he had been cleared of any wrong doing in his girls death, but he still faced disciplinary action for them going as far away as they went and staying as late as they stayed.

But then, he didn't really need to worry, since he knew that AlaHanDrea could show video of exactly what transpired and adolescent males were rarely faulted for chasing tale.

He didn't care though, it didn't really phase him.

Nothing really got through to Dane, he just sat & stared.

Athena refused to leave his side. Her and King Neptune were the only ones allowed to see him.

Alahandrea completely understood, but would sit and focus on him, sending him as much love as she possibly could, in hopes that it would help him to heal.

GAIL ASKED THE YOUNG queen about Dane.

Tears rolled down her cheeks as AlaHanDrea told her about the killings.

Gail was totally fascinated by Alahandrea!

As far as Gail was concerned, the young queen was simply spectacular!

"AlaHanDrea, such a beautiful name for such a pretty young lady. I know I'm just a human, but, can I please be your friend? I really like you! I don't really have any friends, not even back home."

AlaHanDrea looked at her for a moment, then held Gail's face in her hands and look deep into her eyes. "Yes, I think I will like to have you as my friend and thank you."

Gail hugged her, which, took her completely by surprise! Most creatures were terrified to hug her, fearing being absorbed.

She decided that Gail didn't know enough about her to be scared and that was possibly a good thing.

"When did you meet Dane, if you don't mind me asking?" Gail asked her.

"I was about 6 months old or so, and Dane was almost 3.

We still lived on Ion 6, where we are from originally.

His sister, Athena, was helping to raise me, since my mother took her own life right after I was born.

One day, Athena brought Dane to the surface with her. I saw him and he saw me and we fell in love with each other!"

"Aaaaah! How sweet!"

"I gave him a golden necklace and he put a crown on my head.

He also put a golden bracelet on my wrist.

He pledged to always love me and I blew spit bubbles, bounced on my butt and laughed!"

Gail had to laugh when she said that! "Oh, how totally sweet! And the two of you have been in love ever since?"

"Yes," she said, showing off her ring, necklace and earrings.

"Dane gave me these as his promise to always be mine, since he had to have room to grow, see other girls that he could have sex with and all that kind of stuff. I'm still way too young for that kind of stuff!"

"Oh, well, right! Of course you are! Heck, I'm just now becoming of age myself."

"Oh, you're still a virgin?"

"Yes, I am! That's why I got put in the food wagon! I refused to allow the ugly bastard that bought me from my father touch me."

"I'm glad it was Danalli that found you, then. Otherwise, you'd be dead right now. You're really lucky it was Danalli, too!

He's verified in Virgin duty! Make sure you tell him that you're still a virgin!"

"Virgin Duty?"

"Ya, Dragons receive training in sex, romance and all that stuff. They go to school to learn about it all! And Danalli specialized in Virgin Training."

"Really? Oh how cool is that!"

"Oh ya, dragons take the art of sex very seriously!"

"Wow, and humans call Them Beasts! From what I'm seeing, humans are the beasts!"

"Dragon kind are very sophisticated creatures. They are hopeless romantics.

Dragons posses great skills in things such as dancing, music, all sorts of things.

They like dressing up all fancy and socializing.

They are very acrobatic dancers and take roller skating to new heights! They were taught to roller skate by my creatures. The ones who came with me from Ion 6.

My creatures also shape shift.

I will have to introduce you to my Leon.

He is a giant, winged lion king.

Well, right now, he is a prince."

"Really? Oh wow! I didn't know all of that!"

"Why would you know? You didn't hang out in the wilderness."

"True."

"Hello my Queen, I see you two have been getting acquainted," Danalli said as he entered the cave.

He walked over and bowed in front of his young queen, then kissed her hand.

"Gail is very pretty, Danalli, and very lucky that it was you that got her.

She's as pure as pure can be!

It would have been a shame for her to have died, having never felt the touch of a man!"

The look on Danalli's face was priceless!

Alahandrea vanished.

Danalli started laughing, then created a marble dance floor. When Gail looked back at Danalli, he was wearing a tuxedo!

Gail felt a change in herself and looked at her reflection in the wall mirrors.

She couldn't believe the exquisite gown she was wearing and was amazed at her hair and jewelry.

Danalli giggled and said, "thanks AlaHanDrea!!"

"Ya, thanks Girlfriend!" Gail said out loud.

The music began to play. Danalli took Gail's hand and spun her on the dance floor. She could see that her new friend didn't exaggerate ...

Danalli could tell he'd have to be easy with Gail, as far as throwing her around. He toned it way down for her.

Gail felt like she was in a fairy tale!

She had no idea that her dress was made for the bottom to be torn off, so it surprised her when Danalli spun her and ripped the long skirt off of her, revealing the wispy skirt of her leotard.

Gail was surprisingly accomplished at dancing, so, Danalli lifted her up over his head and was surprised when she did an acrobatic move over his head! He brought her back down to the floor and this time when he spun her, she performed a stunt that took Danalli completely by surprise. She did flips back to him, landing by putting her legs around Danalli's waist and her arms around his neck.

"Nice. Very nice, especially for a virgin girl," he teased, then gave her a quick kiss, followed by a passionate kiss that made her heart skip a beat!

"Gail, my sweet precious Gail. I plan to love you like none other! Do you think you can love a beast?"

"I already do love a beast. I also love the man that he is! You, sir, are more than I ever even dared to dream!

You, are my handsome prince!

But more! Much more!

I thought I was put in a cage to die, but I was born when you took me from my cage."

Danalli kissed her again, this time, he caught her in his arms as she lost consciousness.

He laid her sedated body up on a table and placed her feet in stirrups after removing all clothing.

Danalli was very careful and gentle when he removed the hymen.

That was the part that was hard on him!

He got his first view of her beautiful parts, but could not do anything other than gently remove the hymen in a removal procedure, using special instruments.

Removing the hymen as painlessly as possible was considered a mandatory part of a young woman's growth.

When he was done, he clothed her, scooped her up in his strong arms and carried her to her cage to put her to bed.

She woke up the next morning, alone in her cage.

Danalli dreamed of Dane all night long, so, he headed under the sea to pay the young prince a visit.

He was prepared to argue with Neptune, if need be, but received no argument from him.

"Prince Dane, I dreamed of you last night." He walked over and took Danes hand in his hand, connecting with the young prince.

King Neptune almost barged in the room when he heard Dane break down crying, but he resisted.

It seemed that King Neptune had actually dreamed about this very situation, so he stepped back and stayed out of the way.

About an hour or so later, he heard laughter coming from the room and for the first time since the killings, he knew he had his son back!

Athena had only been gone for a short time and for the first time since the incident occurred, but during that short time she was gone, a miracle happened! a miracle named Danalli.

Dane still had some healing to do, but he was well on his way to being better.

Keithen and Braynar had custody of Bob, which, meant that the little Queen had to also deal with Bob!

Chapter 24

T rials and Errors

BOB WAS A UNIQUE CREATURE, to say the least.

He could shift to what ever creature he was with.

Unlike a mimic, he would look like the same species, but had his own individuality.

Mimics look at you, then look like you!

As much as everyone enjoyed Bob, they were all still pretty upset with the humans!

Continuing to try to develop weapons against dragon kind was a cardinal sin!

The heartless human scientists also dumped their failures, as if living creatures were disposable!

The creation of life carries with it certain responsibilities... It just does!

All Lives Matter!

It wasn't just that the scientists dumped the creatures, they dumped them in Drakonia!

AlaHanDrea was taking their attempts to recreate a creature like her, as a personal attack!

It is said that being copied, or imitated, is a sincere form of flattery, but baby girl didn't see it that way.

However, she did enjoy her time spent with Bob. In a way, she felt kin to him... As if he were a brother, something she never had, not to her knowledge, anyway.

"Ala Han Drea"

"Yes, Bob?"

"Ala Han Drea, Nanner, Nanner,"

"I love you, too, Bob."

"Bob."

"Yes, Bob, I'm glad that you came here."

"Gail, Nanner Nanner Gail,"

"I know Bob, but Gail belongs to Danalli and he loves her very much!"

"Bob Bob."

"I know you do, Bob, but Gail is Danalli's. He will be sad without her. And yes, I know that she named you, but she has to be a friend and leave it at that."

"Bob"

"I know it's not, Bob, but that's just the way it is."

"Uh, humph... Bob..."

"Well, right, and someday you will meet the right one and you will love her even more than Gail."

"Uh huh hummm, Bob..."

"Right, now get some sleep, we have a long day tomorrow."

"Bob."

"Good night, Bob."

"Hmph, kiwi kiwi good night Bob!"

"Too bad, now go to sleep!"

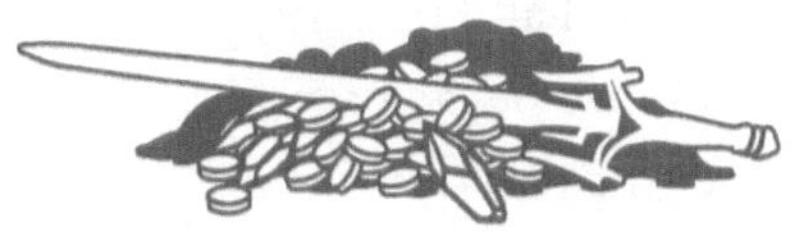

"ALAHANDREA, ARE YOU asleep yet"? Keithen asked as quietly as he could.

"I'm awake. What's up?"

"I can't sleep."

"Would you like some nectar?"

"Yes, please. Do you feel like chatting for a bit?"

"Sure, Keithen, I'll be right down."

"I'm sorry for disturbing you like this, thanks for the nectar."

"I'm always here for you, Keithen. What's going on ?"

"Life."

"I'm sorry, but, you're going to have to be just a bit more specific..."

"I don't even know, tiny one. But besides all of that stuff, I have
Some things for you. Gifts from the belly of the mountain..."

Keithen pulled a small bag out and put it on the table.

"Keithen, I don't quite know what to say!

Thank you!

Oh! Wow!

These are simply gorgeous!

Oh, Keithen, they are magnificent!

I've never seen stones like these before!"

"I hoped you'd love them. Like you, they are quite rare and breathtakingly gorgeous! "

"Oh, Keithen," she said, blushing.

"It's hard to believe that you are only 9 years old!

It seems like only yesterday that you were only 6 years old.

Before we know it, you will be all grown up.

I'm here tonight to make my intentions known.

I fully intend to court you, once you are of age.

You have been a part of my life every day for the last 3 1/2 years.

We have seen both good and bad times.

We have even flown into battle together.

Baby girl, I... I love you already!

I cannot imagine my life without you in it!

You are so special!

So unique!

Others desire to make you their own.

I want to share living with you in my life, not own you...

You are not a girl to be possessed by any man.

I know this already.

Still, once you are ready, once you come of age... Oh, my sweet, precious baby girl!

May I see your crown please?"

She removed her crown and handed it to him, she was speechless!

Keithen pressed the stones into her tiny crown...

Then set it back on her head, kissing her on her forehead.

"Please know that I am right here, waiting for you to become a woman, while still enjoying the girl that you are!

I love you, my queen. I honestly love you."

"Is this why you couldn't sleep?" She asked after finally finding her voice.

"Yes, it is. Mostly..."

"Keithen, I've loved you since the first time I set eyes on you!

Of course I love you, already!

I love Braynar and Danalli, too!

And Leon...

Each in a different, but special way.

I never want my life to be without you in it!

All of you!

Dane, too!

Y'all are my world!

Dane and I have a very special love for one another and always will.

He will get better some day, I just know he will!

However, Dane is a mer, & mers don't pair like others.

He is still my special love.

You were my first friend on this planet...
My first heart throb on this planet.
You, Braynar and Danalli are the center of my universe!
But Keithen, you...
You are my heart in so many ways!
I know that I will love being courted by you!"
"It does my heart good to hear you say that!
AlaHanDrea, I realize that you are only 9 years old, but would you like to go to the ball with me?

Now, I know that you go to bed early, and that's o.k. There's another female that would like to go with us and she will stay up late with me, but, we'd both like for you to go as my date, with her as the chaperone."

"Really? Wow, really? Am I not too young to go?"

"I am the future king, I say you are not too young. Not as long as you have a chaperone."

"Yes, I'd love to go to the ball with you. Thank you for asking me. Only, no mushy stuff!

I'm much too young for kissing mouths!"
"I promise to keep all kisses to your hands, or head."
"Well, o.k. then, I'd really love to go!
Are we going to dance?"
"Well, of course we are."
"O.k. it sounds like fun!
When is this ball?
"Tomorrow night."
"O.k., sounds like fun!
Keithen, I LOVE my crown!"
"I'm glad!
It looks stunning on you! Good night tiny one."
"Good night."
"Bob, hey Bob, it's me, Braynar, where are ya man?

Come on now, Bob, don't be like this!

Dude, men don't have to be invited to a ball!

All men are automatically invited to a ball!

Women have to be escorted or invited!

It's a given that men are going!

You shouldn't have to be invited!

You're a man!

Now, stop being so sensitive, shift to man state and come out here!

Come on now, bro, come on out here!"

"Hello Braynar, you called me bro!" Bob sighed.

"There you are! Bob, all men are automatically invited to a ball.

No one was leaving you out!

I brought you a tuxedo and even took the liberty of arranging for a date for you!

Don't look like that, Bob, she's gorgeous!"

"Really? She's really Gorgeous?" Bob asked.

"Bob! Wow! Listen to you! You can speak the language!"

"Yes, I had to listen to it for a bit, but I believe I have a pretty good handle on it now!"

"I should say you do! Well, won't your date be impressed with you!

Her name is Princess Taeler, but her friends just call her Tootsie...

She's a rare Beauty!

She's also about to become the new Queen of Hawaiilana ... an island country located off of the western coast, about 30 kilometers out.

Many men wish she would become theirs, but she's looking for someone special, not like anyone else... someone handsome, powerful, but most of all, someone with a heart and that's not all stuck on themselves...

I thought of you, now, I'm glad that I did!

You're perfect, dude!

Here's your clothes.

I will be here to take you to pick her up in a few hours, now get ready.

Uh, Bob, can you dance?"

"I can learn," he said, as he produced a viewing screen and asked Braynar for some memories to watch.

"Well, o.k. then, I will by here in a few hours, then. Be ready!" Braynar told him as he left.

"ALAHANDREA, YOU ARE going to the ball with a prince! We must get you properly dressed!" Matilda, the fairy, said.

"Matty, I'm tired of being so tiny.

If I am to dance with a prince, I cannot be so small."

"Then, go ahead and be yourself," Matilda told her.

"AlaHanDrea, Now is as good a time as any. They're going to find out sooner or later anyway. Why not stun them this evening, and go looking like the beautiful young lady that you are.

So elegant & beautiful. ...

So go in your own size." Princess Brandy chimed in.

Princess Brandy was the kind of fairy that tried to stay to herself, really, keep her nose out of other people's business, but, she couldn't resist putting her own two cents worth in.

The tiny fairies hid the beautiful, young Queen, when they heard her prince showing up to pick her up for the ball.

They told him to wait a minute, then made a big deal of presenting her to them. They had her hidden a little ways back so that she'd have to walk up to him a good little bit.

AlaHanDrea finally emerged.

The look on her handsome princes' face was one of total surprise!

Every step the young lady took, she got bigger, until she reached her full size, a couple of steps before reaching her date.

"Wow!

I don't know quite what to say!

Have you always been this big?

I mean, I've always known you were beautiful, for what I could see, because you were so tiny, but now that I see you full size, you are absolutely amazing!"

AlaHanDrea blushed, "thank you Keithen.

I wasn't trying to deceive anyone, I promise.

You have to understand, even though I can defend myself, I didn't want to have to kill creatures for getting wrong with me.

There are men that would harm a little girl, or try to harm a little girl and I don't like having to take someone's life unless I feel I have to.

I didn't want to have to take someone's life for trying to do things to me that I'm much too young for, or things that I didn't want done to me. I didn't/don't want them to even try.

I do hope you understand that I was only trying to protect other creatures, by keeping myself so tiny.

I'm revealing my size at a terrible age to be doing so, truthfully.

But it's hard staying so small all the time, especially when there's something that I really, really want to do, with someone I truly care about.

I just hope that there's not a high price to pay, by me or anyone else, for my having made the decision to come out as I truly am.

I pray that my desires are not over riding my good sense."

"I don't blame you one bit for making the decision to stay small for so long. But you know, eventually, everyone's going to find out anyway.

You're right, you're not like anyone else, especially like other little girls, because, they're not nearly as bright as you are.

You are so grown up, to be so young!

I know grown ups that aren't as grown up as you are!

Girl you are nothing short of amazing!

Not only that,

You look incredible!

I love your choice in gowns!

So sophisticated, yet, so youthful.

Very appropriate for a good young lady!

That dress is incredibly sexy when you take the jacket off... sweetheart, that short jacket is beautiful!

Just barely covering your shoulders the way it does and your shoulder gloves are lovely!

You are just so beautiful!"

"Ah, you're making me blush."

"I speak the truth.

Ya know, I love your crown, but, I brought you something to wear, instead of your everyday crown."

Keithen produced the most beautiful Rose gold, Gold and white gold, lace design, jewel encrusted crown... Tiny like she used to be.

Keithen smiled, then used his magic to properly size it for her, before placing it on her head.

It stood tall in the front, then gradually tapered down to about 3 inches high to complete the circle.

The crown sparkled the prettiest colors, reflecting the brilliant reds and gold's of her long, full, curly hair.

The tiny fairies rushed over and fixed her hair around parts of her crown to keep it secure, just in case she should get thrown around while dancing.

His being so close to her like that, made her feel things she had never felt before!

He looked down into her beautiful eyes, then kissed her softly, before taking a step back.

That kiss had taken both of their breath away for a moment.

Much to her surprise, the young queen felt a tingle of electricity when he kissed her.

She felt kinda strange, almost dizzy.

"YooHoo!" A voice rang out.

"YooHoo! Keithen, AlaHanDrea! Oh, there.... Oh wow! Oh wow oh wow oh wow!

No wonder she needs a chaperone!" Cathey Ann said as she walked over to the couple.

"Queen AlaHanDrea, this is Princess Cathey Ann, heir to throne of Victorein, a kingdom located in the Southern Hemisphere. Her family is the reason for this ball." Keithen said, introducing them.

"It's very nice to meet you, Princess Cathey Ann. You are a very beautiful Princess!"

"Thank you, Queen AlaHanDrea. It's very nice to meet you as well. I look forward to this evening. I love your gown!"

"Thank you, my fairies made it for me."

"Well, Ladies, Shall we go?

What a lucky man dragon I am! Escorting two of the most beautiful women in the known world!"

"Well, c'mon then Stud, let's go turn some heads!"

Cathey Ann said, taking his elbow with her hand.

Chapter 9

The fairies hurried over to stop AlaHanDrea from leaving before they got a chance to put her cloak on her.

"AlaHanDrea! AlaHanDrea, wait!" Brandy called out.

A small swarm of fairies flew over to her with the most beautiful white cloak!

The edges of the entire cloak were trimmed in plush white fluffy fur, hood and all!

She stood there while they wrapped the cloak around her, then held the bottom of it up so it wouldn't drag the ground.

Fairies also picked up the back of Cathey Ann's extra long gown to keep it up off of the ground as well.

They used their magic to produce cloaks for Keithen & Cathey Ann, holding up the back of theirs as well.

A swarm of drummers and fairies playing an array of instruments, to include symbol players, went in front of them, like a small parade.

Led by a parade of fairies, all three couples were on their way.

Braynar's date would be joining them when they passed her home on their way in.

"If y'all don't mind my asking, why all the pomp and circumstance?" Keithen asked.

"Prince Keithen, AlaHandrea, Queen AlaHanDrea, is going out for her first time as a young lady!

This is referred to as a Coming out party!

She is to be presented to the public tonight!

When you arrive, you will pause and stand at the edge of the dance floor, then wait until you are announced.

Then, step out slowly... Pause, allow us to remove your cloaks, one at a time.

After your cloak is removed, take 4 steps forward and turn back towards the crowd and us.

You should be facing the back corner of the dance floor.

We will bring the ladies out one at a time, they will take 2 steps forward, we will remove their cloaks, they will face the crowd, wave, then take 2 steps towards you and Danalli and take y'alls arms.

Prince Danalli is waiting for Cathey Ann.

We are presenting Princess Cathey Ann as well.

It's nice that she chooses to chaperone, but she requires an escort to be presented......"

"O.k! Well, glad I asked!"

Both girls just giggled.

The trio froze in their tracks when they ran into Braynar, Bob and Princess Tootsie.

"Wow! What a gorgeous couple!" Keithen said.

"Thank you, Prince Keithen, I'm a very lucky Bob, um, man.

Very lucky, indeed.

She is stunning!

This is Princess Tootsie.

Braynar set this Bob, uuhhh, all up! Set this all up" Bob exclaimed.

"Bob!" Keithen and AlaHanDrea shouted at the same time.

"Oh Bob!

You can speak our language!

Listen to you!

Wow, this is great" AlaHanDrea said excitedly.

"Why are you so excited? You always understand what I'm saying?"Bob asked.

"Because, Bob, I happen to love you very much, man, you're very special to me!

I want only the best for you!

Your life will be so much better now that you can appear human and sound human, too. Good job Bro.

Man, you can be anyone you want to be, can't you, bro?

No matter the species, you can look the part and know the language in almost no time at all, how cool is this?"

"You love me?

I'm very special to you?

I love you!" Bob had a tear in his eye.

"Wow, I have a gorgeous, powerful dear friend!

Braynar called me brother...

Wow, I have a sibling!" Bob was smiling a big ol smile.

Princess Tootsie had a concerned look on her face... Bob turned and stood in front of her and partially shifted, then shifted back.

What she had seen was Bob's top to about boob level and about 50 thin, tube like arms with long sharp teeth in a shallow mouth on their tips.

Then he quickly shifted back to man state.

They explained about the scientists who made him... And why....... They told her how he was treated and how he was just tossed aside and how he mistakenly killed those young ladies when he wanted to hug them.

He hadn't meant to kill them.

He thought they were pretty and wanted to hug them.

That he was clumsy and didn't know how to use his arms around other creatures and still wasn't very good at it.

He told how he preferred to be in any other creatures form, just not his own form.

It was enough to break anyone's heart!

Braynar knew right then and there that something would have to be done to help him learn to love himself as he really was, naturally.

No creature should have to hate themselves.

Then, Bob provided a short demonstration of his power......

The smile on Tootsie's face, meant that she could appreciate a creature like Bob.........

It didn't hurt that he shifted into a tall, incredibly muscular and handsome, as well as powerful, humanoid male!

His story was a sad one, but Bob was far from sad!

He was strong and powerful! Just the way Tootsie wanted him, sensitive but all powerful!

There was nothing wrong with being both strong and sincere!

It was a great combination as far as Tootsie was concerned.

He was a far cry from any of the men that she had met so far... Well, all but 1...

He was just what the doctor ordered to cure what was ailing her!

Bob was really enjoying the vibes he was getting from Tootsie!

She felt so sincere!

Braynar's lady was thrilled with being picked up by a fairy parade!

The white cloaks put an even bigger smile on her face, if that was even possible.

"Prince Braynar and Princess Jasmine"

Came over the speaker, so Braynar and his date walked up to the edge of the dance floor. The booming voice announced, "Presenting His Highness, Crowned Prince Braynar!

Braynar took his forward steps and waited as the fairies fluttered in front of him, removing his cloak so that it hung in front of him for a moment, before being yanked away to reveal the Handsome Prince... He waved and the crowd went wild with applause.

"Presenting His consort, her highness, the Beautiful Princess Jazmine!"

Cheers, whistles and applause rose up as the fairies yanked away her cloak to reveal a gorgeous Princess, smiling and waving at the crowd .

She took Braynar's arm and they stepped to the side.

"Presenting, the handsome Crowned Prince, Danalli!" The crown cheered and whistled....

"Presenting for the first time Anywhere, Her Highness, Crowned Princess, Cathey Ann!" The crowd got louder when Cathey Ann's cloak was yanked away.

"Presenting for the first time anywhere, His majesty, King Bob!"

The cheering and applause continued as Princess Tootsie walked out, "Presenting, his consort, the Beautiful, Crowned Princess, Tootsie Taeler!"

The sound of the applause and whistles rose to new heights when her cloak was yanked away!

She Waved and curtsied, then took Bob's arm and stepped off to the side...

"Presenting for the first time anywhere, the one! The Only, Baby Queen! QU E E N ALA HAAAAN DDDRRRRREEEEEAAA!"

A hush fell over the crowd as the fairies brought a figure under a white cloak out onto the floor. The announcer said the baby queen, but who ever stood below that cloak was bigger than any 6 inches high!

The fairies yanked the cloak away and not a sound could be heard past an initial gasp... Then, all of a sudden, a roar began to rise up... Cheers, whistles, hooting and hollering and applause rose up to deafening levels!

AlaHanDrea held her arms up high in her victory stance and the crowd went wild!

She stood on stage, with her butt length red and golden curls flowing down her back, crown sparkling in the nightlight, dressed so elegantly, arms in the air, full sized for the first time!...

The click of cameras almost drowned out the sound of the crowd!

Keithen took her hand and gently spun her towards him. The music began and all 4 couples began dancing.

Bob was doing pretty good dancing, but when Braynar and Danalli began getting all fancy, he became distracted, but, once they were through, he took Tootsie into his arms, holding her close, then began dancing with her like a professional that had been dancing with her as his partner for years!

He held her up over his head, tossed her in the air and caught her with great ease...

They danced beautifully together!

The Lions and other Big Cats, Bears, Wolves, Owls, Eagles, Fairies, Unicorns, Horses, Pegasus, Centaurs, etc ... Top royalty showed up, as did the 15 sisters and their husbands.

AlaHanDrea knew what was coming next!

The real show was about to begin!

The acrobatic dancers on wheels were about to begin!

Dragons could be seen putting wheels on their feet in preparation ...

It was about to get real!

Different creatures were taking turns going up and singing while the dancers skated... Then AlaHanDrea froze as she heard the most beautiful voice...

I'm a boy that loves a girl the way this boy loves his girl that loves the boy that loves her, the way a boy is supposed to love a girl who love him.....

AlaHanDrea sang...I'm a girl who loves a boy, who is in love with his girl the way a boy is supposed to love a girl who loves him.... Together they sang, and when we are grown , and are on our own, I will love you the way a woman loves the man in love with the woman who loves him, I will love the woman the way a man loves a woman whose in love with the man who loves her... And when we grow old and our stories get told, they'll sing about a boy who loved his girl that was in love with boy who loves her and that boy is me, oh can't you' see, that girl is me!!!"

Everyone has stood perfectly still as the two young loves sang to each other, slowly walking over to each other as they sang...

"Dane! Oh, My Precious Dane!"

"My Beautiful Queen!"

Dane took her hands, gazing into her eyes. He pulled her close and softly kissed her lips.

Aaaaahhhhhhhh! Could be heard raising up from the crowds., Then soft applause....

Dane twirled her and they began dancing. They paused, used magic to put on skates and it was on!

Her and Dane began showing the grown ups what they were made of! She'd do a handstand on Danes hands as he held them high above his head, then she'd do the splits while she was up there!

The two had a blast!

Everyone watched as they had the time of their young lives!

Danalli got to go pick up his actual date early and Keithen and Cathey Ann got to be chaperones...

Cathey Ann kept taking real good looks at Keithen... The first time they had met, they were babies! He had filled out quite nicely as a man!

Maybe her mother was right...

Keithen sure was growing into a very handsome, muscular, tall and sexy man! Not to mention his singing voice!

A girl could sure do worse!

Everyone was talking about Queen AlaHanDrea and Prince Dane...

How they fell in love before she was even a year old...

how when Dane told her he loved her, she bounced on her butt, giggled and drooled all over her belly....

How she fussed when Dane had to go...

Everyone talked about them being married at first site.

Bonded since shortly after birth...

How Dane knew when he first saw her, that she was the girl for him...

Their song was coming to an end, Dane took her by the hand and began skating away with her. He used his magic to make a skate friendly hallway off of the stage, then spun her around into his arms and held her close... Looking her in the eyes....

I love you, AlaHanDrea! He touched her cheek and kissed her forehead...

"I will be so glad when you grow up!"

She used her magic to age herself, so, he used his magic to age himself, too.

They weren't in a private area.

They stared at each other, then he pulled her back close, paused a moment, then bent down and kissed her for real...

She kissed him back, for real... She melted in his kiss... He lifted her up in arms and began spinning with her, holding her... They began laughing when spinning, then they vanished!

Keithen and Cathey Ann Panicked! It may have looked like they made themselves vanish, but Keithen just didn't think so! He felt in his soul that something was amiss!

Chapter 10

Finding Dane and AlaHanDrea, became a full time gig for everyone.

The kids had somehow vanished and right in front of everyone!

They just stopped being there!

But how?

Bob was beside himself!

He kept going back and sniffing the area around where they had vanished.

He felt something there, but couldn't pinpoint what exactly it was!

All he knew was that he had to find her!

Bob was afraid of finding Dane, but he didn't allow that to stop him.

He shifted into a smaller version of the man state him and began spinning on that same spot.. faster, then faster...

When he stopped, he was standing in a strange place!

Everything looked kind of distorted and wavy.

Bob was afraid to move from the spot he was in, afraid he'd become lost if he even took 1 step...

"AlaHanDrea! Dane! AlaHanDrea! Dane! Can you hear me?" He shouted.

Bob heard a distorted yes coming from somewhere far away.

He began singing as loudly as he could, while holding perfectly still on that spot, afraid to even lift his foot!

The terrified Bob could occasionally hear fragments of their voices, continuing to sing as loudly as he possibly could!

The terrified but determined creature competed with himself, to see how high pitched he could sing and for how long he could hold it....

Singing as loudly as he could sing, for what seemed like hours, before he began seeing glimpses of them!

They'd fade out, then he'd see them and they'd vanish again, getting a little closer each time.

When he'd catch a glimpse of them, he'd get motivated to sing longer, louder, higher...

The kids were getting close enough that he wanted to reach out and grab them, but he somehow knew that they'd all be lost if he did and he held tight to that spot!

Bob patiently waited until they too, were on the spot with him, then he wrapped his arms around them and began to spin in the opposite direction they had been spinning, when something began wrapping around all three of their legs and arms, growling, roaring and sounding terrifying!

Bob partially shifted and began chomping away at what ever it was that had a hold of them!

He used all of his arms and bit the fire right out of that creature!

He was tearing it up, but remaining on his spot and holding the young couple as tightly as he could with his human arms...

One of the things wrapping around the kids got a bit close and AlaHanDrea struck it, injecting it with venom!

It screamed in agony!

More of the things began grabbing at her, she bit as many as she could before running out of venom.

Thankfully, she could still shoot laser beams at them!

But for every one that fell away, it seemed 2 or 3 more would take it's place!

Bob began spinning again, while chomping and biting at everything that tried to pull the kids away, while AlaHanDrea shot laser beams non stop, trying to blast Dane free!

Her and Bob managed to free Dane! Bob tossed Dane straight up in hopes that he'd land back up where he was supposed to be!

Getting AlaHanDrea loose would be another thing altogether!

With Dane out of the way, Bob and AlaHanDrea went after the viny things imprisoning them, with a whole new revived energy, determined to free themselves from that hellish place.

Bob found a use for his 50 plus arms with teeth that day!

It took every single one of his arms, as well as every drop of strength Baby Girl had, to successfully free themselves and get safely back home!

Relief flooded through both of them when they surfaced & saw Dane being tended to by his father..

Someone had seen Bob spin and vanish!

They waisted no time sounding the alarm!

Applause rang out from the crowd when Dane came flying up out of the hole!

Neptune jumped to catch his son!

Fortunately, the distraught king had been standing very closely to the place they had all disappeared from and was able to catch his son!

When Bob surfaced with AlaHanDrea, the applause rang out even louder than before!

King Neptune, King George, Mr Jax and KingRaynar were all there!

Athena and even Mitchin were there!

Bob created a huge plug of sorts, placed it on that exact spot and spun it like crazy, then smashed it with a huge, giant hammer...

A fence was placed around the spot to keep everyone away from It!

Standing on the spot made you begin to spin, then something sucked you in! And just like that, you were gone!

Healix quickly checked AlaHanDrea and Dane out for damage before turning his attention to Bob.

AlaHanDrea stood up on a table and spoke out with a microphone,

"May I please have everyone's attention?

Dane and I would both be dead right now, if not for my dear friend, King Bob!

There were horrible creatures in that weird place, creatures I was unable to defeat without also killing Dane and I.

Bob used his natural shape to save our lives!

Tonight, Bob's my Hero!

Something very strange lives in someplace very strange!

That place is like none other!

My power was restricted, at best!

My strength was restricted!

I felt actual fear!

For the first time in my life, I feared losing my own life!

I've thought I might die before, I just never feared dying before.

That place is not natural!

Whatever it was in there, it had a great deal of company!

We MUST find out what and why it is!

It's not right to destroy something without having as much information as possible, beforehand, when possible to do so without endangering ourselves and others.

However, I don't mind admitting that I'd rather not be counted in the discovery crew...

Where's Mitchin?" The young queen asked.

BRAYNAR WENT UP TO Bob, "Bro, I need to see you! First of all, thanks for rescuing the kids! Man, you are amazing! It was your natural

self that saved those kids! Naturally, you are amazing! It's high time you learn to accept who, what and how you really are!"

"But, but, Braynar," he stuttered...

"Trust me, Bob, Markus, trust me, please. It'll be alright. You just need to train yourself to learn to control all of those arms of yours!"

"But... but... but...I'm hideous!"

"No, you are not hideous! You are perfect! Just the way you are! Sure, you look frightening, so do I, and look how magnificently handsome I am!" He said with a smile. "A smart person fears us both! That doesn't mean we aren't handsome fellas!

Bob, uh, Marcus, Mark, I love ya, man! Your the brother of my heart! I knew the moment I first saw you, that you were a very special part of my life from that moment on."

"You know my name," Bob said with a tear in his eye. "I don't know what to say, Braynar! I must admit, when I first saw you, I wanted to absorb you, truthfully. I wanted to possess all that you are. Now, I'm glad that I didn't."

"O.k, I'm going to take that as a compliment... well, now, if we're through with all of the mushy stuff, what say we get started on learning to appreciate you in your natural form, ya ready?"

"Ready as I'll ever be, and Braynar, thanks man. I love you, too!"

Chapter 11

Merrill was from a long line of wizards.

They'd all lived on the island for as long as anyone could remember or history recorded.

His section of mountains was referred to as Wizards Keep.

Merrill's castle was on the highest peak of the tallest mountain.

As much as the well seasoned wizard hated to admit it, he was going to have to form an alliance with the Dragons.

It was the only way!

He'd tried everything else, to no avail.

The pirates continued to raid, ravage and pillage.

Once his mind was made up, he went to see Princess Tootsie, after all, she was friendly with them... Of course, he had no idea that Tootsie was a Dragon... She wasn't big on revealing...

The Queen was feeble and on the verge of relinquishing her throne to her daughter, still, Tootsie was already running the kingdom.

"Your highness, you have a friendship with dragon kind, I implore you to set me up a meeting at your earliest convenience. Please your majesty, I'm pleading with you."

"If an audience is what you desire, you shall have it at once," Tootsie answered him.

"Prince Braynar will see you now," she told Merrill.

"Thank you so much!" He said before he vanished.

"To what do I owe the pleasure of your company, wizard," Prince Braynar asked the nervous man that stood before him.

"Great one, we are suffering pirates!

They Rob us of the food offerings we have for you and your flocks.

They take your food and turn them into loyal pirates!

Their numbers are growing very large!

The murderous thieves are become extremely difficult to deal with as they grow stronger.,"

His nervousness was showing, but then, who wouldn't be nervous, standing in front of the largest, strongest, most vicious Dragon on Taurus 9...

Braynar felt bad for the man. He gave the situation a little thought, then shifted right in front of Merrill!

"What kind of magic is this?" The wizard asked.

"It's Dragon Magic! We are not the heartless beasts we are made out to be. Quite the contrary," Braynar explained, as he poured 2 goblets of nectar wine.

" It took courage for you to come here like this. You impress me, wizard."

"This nectar wine is absolutely delicious! Wow! Yum!"

"Ya, it's most folks favorite..."

"Thank you for sharing it with me and thank you for listening to me,"

"I'm glad you brought this problem to us. We will handle the pirates.

Gladly.

The boys and I could use a little sporty fun..!"

———————————

When Merrill returned, it was with an agreement between him and the dragons...

Soon, those pirates would come to fear Merrill and his people!

All of the islands off of the mainland, were equipped with gongs and were considered Dragon Friendly.

Some, more so than others.

After landing, dragons would strike the gongs to alert the Islanders to their presence.

Food wagons were then delivered to the waiting giant, fire breathing reptiles...

This had become a practice to try to entice the dragons to fly in no further... Protecting the mainland... Somewhat...

Sinners still had to be shipped to the islands....

Piss off the dragons and they would fly over the mainland!

That was a very bad thing to have happen!

Crops got burned, entire villages would get burned...

It wasn't pretty.

But...Dragons were not without compassion.

Not as a rule.

Now, Occasionally, they would perform what they called a cleanse...

They'd take out entire cities when the cities crime got out of control.

The Dragons saw it as them doing a public service, consuming the sinners and undesirables.

Merrill had never been the enemy of Drakonia, be he wasn't exactly on their friends list either.

Still, these pirate HAD to be stopped!

They'd steal food shipments and keep them as loyal recruits, loyal because they were still alive!

Depriving dragons of their rightful due!

The dragons HAD to be told!

Otherwise, innocent ones would pay the price!

Even Still, he felt very strange about inviting the huge, man eating beasts into their world....

"Hey, Bob, Braynar,

Keithen, Danalli, dudes, c'mon, let's go make some trouble with some pirates!" Craigen shouted as he walked up to where the guys were meeting....

"Sounds like fun, I'm in!" Danalli had his hand raised to be counted.

Then all of the guys raised theirs, too!

"Great! Let's go play!"

"Wait!" AlaHanDrea shouted!

"I want to ride and practice doing tricks, if y'all don't mind...

Danalli was the first one to put a riding harness on, so she readied herself, standing in a clearing.

When she heard the sound of wings, she raised her arms up above her head.

Danalli then flew down and grabbed her in his talons, then threw her high into the sky and caught her on his neck.

She was full sized then, no longer so tiny she could ride on the wind...

A group of princesses, were gathered close by.

They couldn't help but to notice.

They watched her and wanted to be her!

The young ladies watched as AlaHanDrea landed on a dragon, ran down his back and tail, got flipped in the air by that tail... doing aerial stunts, then landing on a different dragon...

Dragons used their magic to put riding harnesses and steering bridals on themselves, to make riding easier for their passengers.

All of the dragons agreed, that they preferred Baby Girl full sized... She was much easier to keep up with!

The girls on the ground called for male brethren, shifted to human state and began mimicking AlaHanDrea's riding style. They began practicing while the royals were off chasing pirates.

While in the air, they overheard Braynar and Danalli speaking telepathically and decided to fly over and offer back up, with the girls on their necks in full armor.

It was a beautiful sight to see!

They arrived on the scene to find the Royal brethren circling high above the ships.

None of them had any idea the pirate's numbers were so great!

The new arrivals joined in the circling and called for more backup!

Within the hour, this sky grew dark, as the dragon's blocked out the Sun!

It was time to attack!

"Brethren, their numbers are great because they've been stealing our food!

Most of those humans belong to us and stink of sin!

Those are our stolen property!

Show no mercy!

Attack!" Braynar ordered.

The dragons lowered their huge circle above the ships and began breathing fire across the circle until they had set fire to every ship in the circle!

The sea was ablaze with burning ships!

As men jumped off of the doomed ships, sharks were waiting on them, making a meal of them.

The screams of the pirates could be heard above all else!

The only sounds louder, were the cheers of the Islanders nearby, as they watched their enemies die.

Dragons began swooping down through the flames to grab up some of the sailers for themselves, as the ships burned.

"AlahanDrea, you must be hungry, too, go get yourself some sailors!" Keithen told her.

"No thanks, I don't swallow seamen..."

Almost every dragon there, began to fall into the water, laughing themselves silly...

"What?

What did I say?" Was her response...

Danalli lost it that time and they, too, hit the water, with Danalli laughing so hard he was almost choking...

———————

"I don't know about the rest of you, but I'm wet and hungry, I'm headed for shore," Braynar told the flock and began swimming like a duck, still laughing, headed for the beach.

The Islanders were confused!

They had watched the dragons defeat the pirates, then, all of a sudden, they began falling from the sky!

Only to begin paddling to shore like ducks!

How odd!

Almost as odd as seeing crown wearing women in full armor, riding on the necks of dragons, with rains in their hands!

———————

AlaHanDrea put the fire out on 3 badly damaged ships and instructed everyone to leave a couple of wounded survivors...

She used her magic to turn the pirate ships flags upside down...

Then, she added Drakonian victory flags to their masts... Sending the smoldering ships out to sea...

As a going away gift, she contacted King Neptune and asked him to be sure the pirate ships made it to someplace where their stories could be told and spread....

3 different places for 3 different ships...

———————

Merrill saw everything from his tower.

"The enemy of my enemy is my friend," he said out loud to himself.

The avenged wizard rushed down to the beach to thank and congratulate his new found allies...

"Prince Braynar! Awesome job! Y'all made that look easy! Thank you very much, your highness."

" We aim to please...

I'm wanting something now.

I wish to have lairs in your mountains.

Full scale lairs." Braynar informed him.

"Well, of course! I wouldn't have it any other way. How many dragons will be residing in the lairs?" He asked, trying not to sound like he was worried about the amount...

"Don't really know yet, does it matter?

We rather like our homes we have, however, our lairs cannot be left unattended, so, we will probably take shifts..." Braynar explained.

He could tell that Merrill knew little of the ways of dragons.

Most humans didn't.

Merrill would soon find out just what Braynar meant, once the mining began...

Islands tended to produce amazing gem stones!

Braynar was real excited about the new mines... As well as the new vacation spot and eatery...

Chapter 12

Time waits for no one.

It seemed like only yesterday that Baby Girl was turning 10, and here she was, close to turning 16! Already!

The Dragon Riders had been practicing their battle moves with the dragons for 6 years at that point and were becoming quite accomplished warriors!

AlaHanDrea was proud that she was the inspiration for the dragon riders to form.

What had started out as a handful of princess's, then numbered in the hundreds!

All Female!

Well, except, of course, for the dragons.

More recruits showed up daily to begin their training...

The Queens each led battalions of troops.

Together, they formed a mighty army!

A true force to be reckoned with!

Leon and the other giant, winged lions, joined in the flying army, with their own Queens riding on their necks.... As did the giant, winged wolves...

All manners of flying beasts joined in...

The dragons honestly loved the other flying beasts, Leon in particular!

That big, ferocious, fearless kitty gained the respect of all creatures!

A huge feast was being held the night before the great ball.

AlaHanDrea sat at the royal table by Isabel.

The feast was an actual sit at the table kind of thing... The dragons were becoming accustomed to cooked food served on plates.

Rhythm drums announced approaching royalty.

It was Prince Leon and his full Entourage, complete with a mini parade...

He walked right up to AlahanDrea

"Your majesty," he said, as he took her hand and kissed it, bowing to her.

If no one has asked you to accompany them to the Ball yet, I would very much love to have you as my date.

Please forgive my late timing in asking.

I'm aware of the fact that I am not the only male showing Interest in you. Be it not for me, to step on any toes...

However, given the lateness of my request, had anyone else desired to take you, surely they would have said something by now."

"No one has asked me And I would absolutely Love to go with you to the Ball!

Thank you for asking me, Leon, I'm looking forward to it."

" Have you heard from Prince Dane?"

"I'm afraid I have not.

His sister stays with him most of the time now.

All I can do is hope and pray. This year marks 6 years."

"I'm so sorry your majesty. I suppose it was just too much trauma, too soon after the other great Traumas...

The killings were very rough on the young prince, only to be thrust into eminent danger once again.

I'm sure he will be alright, my queen.

I do hope that I've given you enough time to secure a chaperone, if not, I'm certain I can make suitable arrangements....." He was interrupted by an annoyed 15 year old queen! "I will have you know,

Prince Leon, that I am no longer a child! I do not require a chaperone to babysit me! However, if you feel that I cannot trust you, then maybe I should arrange for a chaperone..." She said, with a look on her face that spelled trouble!

I'm well aware of the fact that you are now a woman, my Queen.

I will pick you up tomorrow before supper. Until then..." Leon kissed her hand and turned to leave.

Standing at the edge of

the dance floor, looking as beautiful as he'd ever seen her, was Sewella.

Leon had not seen Sewella in several years.

Not since she ran away.

His heart skipped a beat...

He was Ill prepared for running into her.

Leon lost his virginity to her! He thought he had been in love with her.

Nothing like the love he felt for AlaHanDrea, but love...

Only it wasn't really love. It was more like lust mixed with ego.

When she turned up pregnant, Leon didn't know what to say or do. He became very excited about becoming a father, then she vanished!

Now, there she was, standing right there!

He turned as though he had not seen her at all, and quietly left.

The memories of Riley coming up and saying that it was his fault that she left, because HE had fathered her cubs!

Then, Danold came up and said it was HIS fault that she ran off, because HE had impregnated her!

Leon doubted he'd ever forget that kind of hurt.

He'd hoped he'd never have to look at her again.

But, there she was!

Shortly after discovering the other potential father's, Leon ran into Lord Pooky, the Love Dragon.

Pooky talked Leon into attending the love academy, just like the dragon males did...

As it turned out, Leon was very glad that he had listen to the wise Pooky...

His 2 years at the academy began paying off right away...

Still, there she was! And she showed up at the dinner!

Leon tried not to allow it to bother him.

After all,. AlaHanDrea agreed to be his date for the ball!

He was slightly concerned about the date, after all, AlaHanDrea was soon to be 16 years old and was full of raging hormones ..

Still, he preferred she go with him than a male mostly out to score...

Not that he wouldn't enjoy the conquest, but Leon's love for AlaHanDrea was deep and pure.

He knew he was in love with her from the moment he set eyes on her as a baby.

He knew then that he'd always love her.

She was still a Virgin and Leon fully intended to keep her that way,!

Going to the Ball was a big deal, socially.

Many females lost their virginity due to the romance of the evening.

Lord Pooky taught his students to respect a virgin. She must be properly opened before her first sexual experience, otherwise, it was very painful the first few times and could damage the girls drive for the remainder of her life.

Hymen removal procedures were highly recommended, followed by dilators to gently, gradually, open her as painlessly as possible.

That way, her first experience was enjoyable and fulfilling, setting the stage for a healthy sex life...

Leon was really fond of the dragons ways. He agreed with their views and policies, for the most part.

The biggest challenge from the start, was trusting the giant reptiles not to eat kitties..

After all, Dragons were rumored as loving to eat kitties...

Chapter 13

AlaHanDrea was surrounded by Fairies all day long, primping her for the ball.

The last Ball she had attended, Dane showed up and they almost got killed together.

She hadn't seen much of Dane since that night...

Not by her choice, either.

AlaHanDrea tried not to stress over the things she had no control over...

Instead, she opted to focus on the things she could control...

Her mind wandered to Prince Leon...

He was looking really good!

He was filling out!

His voice had gotten deeper bass, his shoulders were wider, muscles were much bigger... he seemed taller, too.

He looked more like a man than a boy!

He was also her date for the evening.

Besides primping, the fairies were teaching the young queen to dance...

She could already dance quite well, but the fairies felt that she needed to learn a few moves for older girls...

It occurred to the excited young lady, that she needed a gift to give to Leon!

She had almost forgotten!

She used her magic to creat an amulet on a heavy golden chain. She instilled the amulet with magical powers and abilities, then wrapped it in a very ornate box.

The gown the fairies made for her was exquisite!

Her hair was part up with the back down and flowing. The front was wrapped into her crown to hold it on throughout the night.

Once again, the fairies adorned her with the white cloak. Only that time, they put it on her before Leon got there.

AlaHanDrea was ready, as well as a bit nervous!

She was anxious about what the night would entail.....

Would Leon try to kiss her?

Would he try to.....

no, not Leon, or, would he?

No, not Leon.

But, why not Leon?

She really hoped he'd kiss her!

"He's here! He's coming down the path!" Brandy the fairy, hollered out in excitement.

"Hello Prince Leon," Brandy said, as she greeted the Prince. "She's ready."

AlaHanDrea walked out wearing the cloak.

"Oh, so, not fair!

May I please see my lovely date?"

The fairies slowly removed the cloak.

"Wow! Oh, Wow! AlaHanDrea, my Queen!

You look Absolutely breathtakingly gorgeous!

Wow!

You look like a full grown woman!

Wow!

You're stunning!￼"

"Oh Leon," she said, blushing. " Here, this is for you. I made it using my magic. I hope you like it!"

"Oh, my sweet, precious baby girl, you didn't need to do all of that, thank you so much.

What a gorgeous box!" He commented.

"The box isn't the gift, Mr. Silly, open it!" She coaxed.

"Oh!AlaHanDrea!

It's magnificent!

Such intricate details! And this chain is exquisite!

The gemstones are just, wow!

Baby girl!

I LOVE it!" He said as he slipped it over his head and around his neck.

"Be kind of careful with it, Leon. It's magical, from My personal magic... It's an amulet of protection.." She cautioned her lifetime heart throb.

"Oh wow, Really?

Oh wow!

I don't quite know what to say!

Thank you!"

He stepped in front of her, tilted her chin up with his finger and kissed her softly on the lips.

Electricity coursed through her entire being!

He kissed her again, a bit more passionately... her first real, true kiss.

She melted in his arms!

"AlaHanDrea, I have waited a lifetime to do this," and he kissed her one more time, taking her breath away for a moment.

It was like magic!

The fairies quickly put the cloak back on her and repaired her lipstick, then picked up the back of her cloak and dress, forming the parade for Leon and his Entourage.

Leon didn't feel right about AlaHanDrea walking, not even a short distance, so, he shifted back to his natural state.

She rode up on his shoulder, with his Entourage in a parade in front of them.

They were a site to be seen!

Of course, the handsome young prince shifted back to man state, wearing his best Tuxedo, once they arrived.

"Announcing, Prince Leon and Presenting Q U E E N Ala...Han...DREA!￼!!

Applause and cheers rose up from the crowds as the couple entered the dance floor.

When the fairies removed the white cloak, whistles rang out at near deafening volumes!

The young queens gown showed off her ample bosomes, slender waist and curvy hips. The dress slit up the front to show off her muscular thigh...

It was more than obvious that she was no longer a child!

Prince Leon and Queen AlaHanDrea danced the first dance around the floor, showing off for everyone, as was customary.

Keithen, Danalli, Bob and Braynar were already in attendance, along with their dates for the evening.

Keithen's date spoke up first," looks like you three are slipping! Kitty done went and poached your little girl!" She teased...

Keithen, Braynar and Danalli we're in awe of the woman she was becoming and more than just a little bit jealous of the kitty.

"Announcing Prince Kai and Princess Katrina!"

"Oh, look Leon, the triplets are here! All fifteen of them!" She barely had the words out of her mouth before skates were on both of their feet!

Leon and AlaHanDrea didn't miss a song!

They stayed on the dance floor having a blast!

After about the 6th song, Leon skated up to the bandstand, so AlaHanDrea followed him.

Leon got up on the stage and took a seat at the grand piano.

AlaHanDrea smiled, got up on stage and sat on top of the piano.

The royal trio decided to join them on stage, and drug Bob up with them...

Bob surprised everyone with his skill playing the trumpet! Keithen had a saxophone and Braynar was strumming a 6 string.. as well as singing backup.

The carefree couple sang several duets together, quite beautifully... with electricity anyone could see, building by the moment!

The band did a great job at keeping up with all of them, too.

When in man state, Leon's wings don't retract.

He actually looks closer to being AlaHanDreas same kind, as just about Anyone could.

They looked beautiful together!

Sewella sat to the side, watching them... Trying to be inconspicuous, un noticed....

AlaHanDrea noticed her, tho. And, the young queen wasn't about to let the woman mess up her special night!

AlaHanDrea was feeling very uneasy. A sense of impending doom slipped it's way in...

Leon finally cought sight of her... He closed his eyes, took a deep breath, then sighed.

"She meant a lot to you once, didn't she?" AlaHanDrea asked.

"Yes, yes she did, once...

I recovered..."

"Are you sure?" She asked her handsome prince, the pain still obvious.

"Time will heal the wounds," was all Leon said.

It began to make baby girl uneasy that the woman kept staring at her. AlaHanDrea did her best to just ignore the woman... But, the woman didn't want to be ignored!

AlaHanDrea had finally had enough and decided to go confront the girl!

Baby Girl got about half way across the dance floor and went flying backwards!

She got up, shook herself off and threw a fireball at that annoying female, barely missing her head.

Guests scattered as AlaHanDrea and Sewella squared off at one another, poised for full battle!

AlaHanDrea screamed her glass shattering scream, sending Sewella flying backwards!

Sewella got up and charged towards AlaHanDrea, only to find herself rolling away on the ground...

AlaHanDrea wasn't used to hand to hand combat, but she was sure ready for it!

Sewella used magic to pop up right in front of Baby girls face and AlaHanDrea punched her hard in the center of the girls face!

She continued punching the female, hard and fast, bouncing the girls head off of a wall she was backed up against, like a boxer punches a speed bag!

That's when AlaHanDrea saw it!

She jumped back away from the thing, and ran over to Leon!

"Leon, it's not who you think it is!

She's not who she's supposed to be!

That's not her!

It's an imposter!

Leon, Sewella's passed on.

That's not her!

The creature inside of her body, killed her!

Threw her right out!

This creature desires to kill you.

It chose a form it thought it could get close to you as...

But make no mistake, it's on a mission and that mission is to make you dead!

You and your parents!

Sewella could tell AlaHanDrea was on to her.

She began to slowly make her way through the crowd in an attempt to escape.

AlaHanDrea locked her gaze on the woman, held her hand out in front of herself and began making the sign for come here, closing and opening her fist... Palm up...

Sewella couldn't help herself, she began moving towards AlaHanDrea, struggling to break free, to no avail...

It appeared that she was voluntarily walking over to her, but she was being pulled....

AlaHanDrea very quickly created another amulet. She had Leon step over and place it around Sewella's neck...

The creature inside of Sewella began thrashing and screaming!

The music stopped and suddenly, all eyes were on AlaHanDrea.

No one had a clue what was going on, that would cause AlaHanDrea to be so aggressive towards Sewella!

They all looked on while AlaHandrea exercised the invader out of Sewella's body.

The creature struggled and thrashed about, then through shockwaves at Leon!

His amulet began to glow and the shockwave bounced backwards towards the sender!

The creature tried and tried to attack Leon. Everything it threw at him, ricocheted back at it!

The amulet was doing its job!

It was Protecting Leon!

Much to everyone's surprise, a dark cloud flowed out of Sewella and her limp body dropped to the ground...

AlaHanDrea rushed over to the body, bent over it, and began blowing into her mouth, as tho she were trying to resuscitate the girl.

Healix rushed over to see what was going on.

AlaHandrea stood up, materialized a bottle and forced the black cloud into the bottle, placed the cork in and marked it deadly poison.

Healix and Raynar loaded the girls body on a stretcher and carried her to a tent.

Leon and AlaHanDrea followed them into the tent.

"AlaHanDrea, you said she was dead, but she's breathing and her heart beats..." Leon asked, feeling confused.

"Because, the body offered a vacancy... With the monster imprisoned, the body was available! So.. rather than allow it to die, I recycled it...

I put my mother in there." She admitted.

"However, it won't be for another day or maybe even as long as 3 days before she is in any condition to see anyone, even me...she will need to be watched every second... a good job for the fairies.

I can trust princess Brandy with the task....

She's the best!

It feels so strange to not have my mother anymore. She's been with me since shortly after I was born... I feel kind of.... Empty...

But for now, we are at the ball! So, let's go ... Have a ball!" She was trying to sound as light hearted as she possibly could.

Truth be known, she didn't really feel that great Anymore

It must have shown and when Leon questioned her, AlaHanDrea told him she was feeling tired and asked him to put up a hut and take her to it please, then collapsed in his arms.

He scooped her up, cradling her like a baby, made a hut appear and took her inside.

Healix was hot on his heals!

Leon laid her on the bed, then stood and looked at her for a moment ... she was just sleeping, but her breathing was shallow ...

Healix had a look of worry on his face.

"Leon, she appears to be depleted...

Dude, I'm sorry, but she's dying..."

"WHAT? But How.... Why?

"The best I can figure out, she used up all of her energy... Dancing... singing... fighting... and finally, transferring her mother... That, in itself, took a huge amount of energy!

Dude, you've seen her eat a storm?

The girl is powerful, true, but she requires tremendous amounts of power to recharge herself.

She calls Bolts of lightening to herself! Many, many bolts of pure electricity! And she soaks them up like a sponge!

The power that is output, the more power is required to sustain it, as well.as.to sustain her.

Big engines require big amounts of fuel...

She ran out of fuel."

"I'd like to be alone with her, please, if you don't mind, and Healix, please don't tell anyone else, not yet... Please." Leon had tears running down his cheeks.

"Take your time, Leon, call me if you uh need me," he said as he stepped out to allow them to be alone.

She was so beautiful!

So desirable!

Leon couldn't resist...

He bent down and kissed her gently on the lips...

She stirred. .

He kissed her again and she began kissing him back!

His kisses seemed to be energizing her! So, he kissed her with more passion.

Heat began to rise between them...

The heat of passion...

AlaHanDrea wrapped her arms around Leon's neck and kissed him back with just as much passion as he gave her...

She let her hand trail down his muscular chest, desire rising up in her with every inch she touched .

AlaHanDrea had not ever touched a man like that before!

Leon kissed her again and she slid her hands inside of his shirt, then down to his zipper.

He stood up and shook his head. Leon's hands were shaking as he poured a glass of water and gave it to her, then excused himself for a moment.

The sound of a glass crashing on the floor made Leon turn around and hurry back into the room.

She was unconscious again and the glass was broken on the floor where she dropped it when she passed out.

Once again her breathing became shallow.

Leon pulled her into his arms and kissed her again.

She began to stir.

The electricity generated through passion was actually feeding her!

He began kissing down her neck and she began to moan and wake up some.

Leon let his fingertips gently trail from her shoulders to her wrist, while quietly telling her how beautiful and desirable she was.

He kissed her again and she put her arms around his neck, kissing him so lovingly...

She gasped when his hand found her breast.

His kisses trailed down her neck to her shoulder while stimulating her breasts.

Baby girl was wide awake and on fire!

In a show of dominance, Leon put her hands above her head and pinned her down while kissing her, placing his free hand under her hips, pressing her against him.

She could feel him through his clothes.

His desire was more than obvious.

The way Leon had her, she would have had to hurt him badly to get free... But she didn't want to break free, she was liking him overpowering her like that...

AlaHanDrea could feel his hesitation... She used her magic to remove the top of her dress, exposing her breasts.

Leon ripped the buttons off of his shirt , dropping it on the ground.

The feel of their bare skin pressed together like that was driving desire to new heights!

Leon held her hips tightly up against himself as he argued with himself.

His hands began finding her places.

She was squirming under his touch...

His skill was undeniably expert level!

He felt her body quake under his touch.

She cried out as wave after wave of sheer ecstasy flowed throughout her entire body for the first time in her life!

She barely had time to breath before he was sending her right back over the top!

Leon finally let her have her hand back and gave her a goblet of nectar wine.

The young prince wanted her so badly he could barely stand himself!

It was taking every drop of self control he had, not to just climb up and have his way with her!

He kept reminding himself, that they were only doing what they were doing, to revive her...

And he was finishing her, to cool the fires he lit to make her well....

He just wasn't having intercourse with her...

She was looking awake enough, so he began to put clothes back on, only to have AlaHanDrea remove them again with her magic.

"AlaHanDrea!"

"Leon!"

"AlaHanDrea! Now, cut that out!"

"Look, Leon. We all have needs, even me!

This needs to happen, I'd really rather it be with you!

But with or without you, it's going to happen!" She told him as she dropped her dress to the floor.

He took a deep breath, grabbed her and began kissing her again...

He stood straight up, lifting her off of the ground, so she wrapped her legs around his waist.

Desire was beginning to override his better judgement.

Leon suspected she was using her magic against him ... he didn't mind it tho, it was feeling so good... Who could blame him if she was using magic...He thought to himself...As long as he wasn't taking advantage...

"No!" He scolded himself.

But she wasn't giving up!

She used her magic to remove his pants!

She was right there!

He put her against the wall, her legs still wrapped around him, things began to happen, when once again, he stopped himself.

This time, he touched her forehead and put her to sleep.

With her fully sedated, he laid her on a stirrup table and called up his Virgin kit.

He numbed her up and performed the hymen removal procedure.

That was not an easy task for him, but totally necessary for her.

It didn't make her ready for sex, not by itself. She'd have to go thru using the dilators to gradually open herself first, to prevent pain and possibly damage.

Once the procedure was compete, he used magic to dress her and then erased part of her memory.

Using his magic, he restored her clothes and hair before reviving her.

He told her nap time was over, it was time to go back to the ball!

The three royal brothers were relieved to see them return . For a minute there, they thought the giant kitty cat was going to pick her flower!

They were relieved to see that she was still a virgin... had the big kitty picked her flower, she'd have been walking differently...

"Leon, I feel strange, kind of empty... Ah! LEON! My mother is Gone! Leon! My Mother!"

"Calm down, sweetheart, calm down.

Do you not remember? Your mother is going to have a new life thanks to you!

Listen, I need to take you home.

You need your rest.

You passed out on me.

We've had a big day, Baby Girl.....A wonderful, big day and a great night! Let's get your cloak and you can ride on my shoulders"

"Well, ok, but, Leon, can we fly for a little while?"

"Anywhere in particular you'd like to go?"

"Yes! Up, up and away...! Just for a little bit..."

"Sure, sweet girl, that sounds really nice, here, climb on,"

The way things had been going and with an attempted assassination, as soon as Leon was in the air, so were half a dozen or more Dragons... The royal guard saw fit to accompany them at a distance...

Gliding through the air was rejuvenating!

Leon smelled it first! A change in the ozone...Undeniably, a storm was brewing!

It was time for most creatures to take cover...

But, It was time for AlaHanDrea to prepare herself for a powerful meal!

Leon headed for the ground, setting her gently on the ground, then took off for cover before the rain began.

The storm was a small one. It didn't really pack much of punch. It did very little in the way of giving her energy level back. Her big kitty could tell she was not yet well ..

"Leon, can I ask a big favor of you?"

"Sure, sweet girl..."

"Spend the night with me...

Please...

I don't want to be alone tonight.

I just want to crawl up in your strong arms...

Close my eyes and dream about us..." She said, yawning.

Leon pulled her close to himself and kissed her so sweetly....

And the Sparks began to fly!

He picked her up in his arms, carried her to her room and laid her down in her bed, then climbed in next to her, with his pajamas already on.

Just the act of him climbing in the bed next her, made her tingle all over!

It took everything the young prince had to control his desires!

He held her close and began singing to her.

It wasn't long before sleep claimed her.

Leon laid there, holding her like he was... With her fast asleep in his arms...

He was imagining what it would be like to be with her...

Chapter 14

When AlaHanDrea woke up to greet the new day, she discovered that she was laying curled up with Leon!

Relief flooded through her when she realized they were wearing pajamas!

It felt extremely nice to wake up in his arms like that.

AlaHanDrea didn't get much physical affection yet.

Most creatures were afraid to get too close to her.

Leon wasn't afraid.

In all honesty, the thought of absorbing him right then and there was crossing her mind... But, he began to wake up.

When he looked down and saw her, he tightened his arms around her a bit and smiled the biggest smile, then relaxed his hold a bit, raised up onto an elbow, gazing into her eyes...

"Please don't get upset for me saying this to you, but, AlaHanDrea, I am very much in love with you... Girl, you start my heart!"

"Prince Leon! Are you still here? Your parents are very worried about you! You are to return home at once! Prince Leon! Your highness, are you still here? You need to get your behind home and meet with your parents at once!" It was the royal guard's!

Leon jumped up out of bed, but before he could get his clothes on, his parents came barging in. Leon stood there in a pair of pajamas, looking guilty as all Hell....

"You were out all night. Your mother flipped out when she saw that your bed had not been slept in!" King Leon Scolded.

"Mother, Dad, I'm so sorry that I worried you! And...No, I didn't, she is still a virgin!

I did not forget who I am!

I'm so sorry that I worried you both," he pleaded...

"Sweet girl, I need to go, my parents need to scold me and I deserve it. I was an irresponsible and thoughtless son.

Soon, I will see you soon!" He bent down and kissed her so sweetly.

"King Leon, before you go, he wasn't trying to be bad and please don't take him from me right now," she pleaded, with a tear in her eyes.

"I have carried the soul of my mother since I was a few days old.

Last night, I separated from her and for the first time, I felt so alone!

I needed Leon last night. I needed him so badly and still do! Please don't take him from me right now..."

The ground began to tremble under her words.

The king and queen looked at one another, then the queen sat on the bed next to AlaHanDrea, pulled the girl over into her arms and began gently rocking her, singing to her and comforting her.

Tears rolled down Alahandrea's face as she drifted back to sleep.

The queen kissed her on top of her head and gently laid her back down.

Then she took her husband's arm and very quietly left the room. They left Leon with her for a bit.

When Baby Girl woke up again, Leon was beside her.

"Good morning, sunshine.

I have a gift for you.

We are going to play a game called 'what if'.

What if we didn't stop ourselves last night."

He pulled a very strange vest of sorts out and had her put it on!

It simulated a pregnant belly. She was to wear the thing both day and night. It was programmed to grow and then get born.

A robot baby would emerge!

"Oh Leon, please don't be so dramatic!"

"Why not? Last night was your very first date, as a woman.

We were getting very carried away. Too carried away, and that's just not o.k.

There's no better way for you to truly understand the consequences, than to do this little exercise, please, trust me, you will thank me later, now, put this on," he coaxed.

Reluctantly, she agreed.

"Leon, this is silly!"

"Just humor me and don't take it off! I promise, you will thank me later."

It seemed the most trending topic for discussion was AlaHanDrea's fake pregnancy.... Everyone had an opinion...

Just like Leon had told her, the belly grew!

And grew!

And grew some more!

She was finding it hard to get up out of chairs and especially hard to get up from hammocks...

Her feet hurt, her back hurt...

The baby finally got born.

The bot baby cried a lot, ate a lot, pooped a lot!

And cried some more!

At the end of two weeks, AlaHanDrea stormed into the lions den looking for Leon, with a crying bot baby in her arms.

She spotted Leon's mother...."pardon the intrusion, your majesty, but this belongs to your son as much as it belongs to me!

Would you mind holding bot baby while I go have a bit of a chat with your boy?"

"Certainly, my son is right over there with his daddy, go on over!" Just as soon as AlaHanDrea was out of ear shot, the queen and her girlfriends busted out laughing, while they tried to get bot baby to shut the Hell up!

"Excuse me, your majesty, I'm so sorry to intrude like this, but I need to speak with your son for a moment, please.

Oh, no, don't get up, what I have to say, I can say in front of you!" She said, with frustration in her voice.

"O.k. Mr. Smarty Pants, I've gone along with this thing and I'm here to tell you something.... I did not get fake pregnant alone! It was your idea, therefore, you made me fake pregnant with a bot baby!

You are the daddy!

And, as such, You, should be sharing in the responsibility!

But are you?

Heck no!

You're over here sitting on your duff while I'm stuck home with a crying and pooping machine!

And...

It won't let me sleep!

Well, daddy, I've had it for two weeks and I think it's your turn to do 2 weeks!"

Other lions in the den quietly applauded her!

"Oh, sweet girl, I believe the points been well made. I will go ahead and decommission bot baby and put her away..."

AlaHanDrea interrupted him, "Oh no you don't! You were 50% of this equation! I did My 2 weeks and now, it's your turn to do 2 weeks! Fair is only fair, Prince Leon! What's the matter, you afraid of the bot baby you created?"

The king spoke up, trying not to crack up laughing.... " ya know son, as much as I hate to admit it, the girl does make perfect sense!"

"But, but... but, Dad!"

"She's right, son! Fair is fair, after all! The pride is watching, it's time to set an example..."

The queen went over and handed the baby to Leon. Bot baby woke up and began fussing!

"Well, I'm outta here! It's nap time for me! Good luck with our child, daddy!" And she was off to get some much needed sleep.

Leon looked at his parents, but before he could say a word, his father grabbed his mother, they both shifted and took off for a good run...

Everybody he looked at would turn and take off before he could say even one word....

He tried to lay bot baby down and just walk off, but an alarm went off, telling on him.

He picked it back up, burped it, changed its diaper and got peed on! Just as he got that all cleaned up and a fresh diaper on it, it pooped so much that poop ran out of the diaper and onto Leon!

He finally got that all cleaned up, bot baby washed up, gave it a fresh bottle, burped it again, twice... then rocked it and sang it to sleep. "Ya, o.k., I've got this...

He no sooner laid bot baby down to nap, a loud crashing sound woke it up and once again, it was screaming and crying..... by the time the sun began to go down, he was exhausted!

With bot baby asleep, Leon decided to have a seat. He just got his feet put up, when a clap of thunder boomed so loudly it made everyone jump! It also woke up bot baby!

"Here, give it to me.... Geeesh...." AlaHanDrea said as she walked into Leon's camp.

"Oh, well, hello there little mommy, nice of you to stop by..." Leon said, sarcastically.....then giggled....

"Leon, I don't expect you to do this for 2 weeks. One day is enough. Go ahead and turn it off."

"No can do, prides watching... the challenge is 2 weeks and 2 weeks is what I have to do! We are setting a precedence..."

"Well, ya know what? 2 parents are better than one. Hand Lilly to me."

"Lilly, huh? What a pretty name! Lilly, I rather like that." Leon took AlaHanDrea by the shoulders, bent down and kissed her the sweetest, most loving kiss... with the baby between them... the interesting thing, was that Lilly didn't fuss when her "parents" kissed.

AlaHanDrea was totally under Leon's 'spell'.

Holding that bot baby between them, caring for it together... was doing something to both of them..... they were bonding on a whole different level....

Another clap of thunder and AlaHanDrea quickly handed the baby over to 'daddy' and perched herself on top of the highest hill, in anticipation of the brewing storm...

Leon watched in utter amazement as the storm rolled in and his beautiful love began calling the storm into herself!

Then, he saw it, but only for a millisecond...

A lightening bolt flashed as she ingested it...

He wiped his eyes... There it was again, too brief to really see good, but it looked as tho AlaHanDrea had a different creature inside of her and was only shifted to look humanoid...

For a brief moment, she looked ... Well, she looked like a cross between a watcher and a dragon!

Leon shuddered at the thought! She was one Hell of a frightening creature in her true form...

Maybe it was for the best that Leon caught a glimpse of her as she truly was! Only, It frightened him beyond words!

He knew from that moment on, that he'd never get carried away again!

The reality that his great love was, in reality, a hideous and deadly, dangerous monster, hit the young prince very hard!

King Leon and his wife had decided to return to see if they could help their son with the fake baby. When they arrived, AlaHanDrea was still on the hill and Leon was staring off into space, unresponsive!

Prince Leon could hear his parents, but he only mumbled incoherently.

The king called for the medicine man to come quickly.

AlaHanDrea finished her after storm pee and noticed a crowd around Leon. When she went to check it out, Leon became hysterical!

His parents had no idea what their son had seen that would cause him to be like that, but they knew it had to do with the baby girl!

"AlaHanDrea, something has happened to frighten our son! He is in a state of shock. We will contact you when we know something, but for now, maybe it would be best if you went home. Leon will be fine. We'll let you know, now, run along..." The queen said to her, dismissing her.

She began to object, but instead, popped out and went home, feeling very confused and rejected.

The queen knew AlaHanDrea was upset when the child vanished like she did! But, she tried not to dwell on it, Leon needed her...

Word of the bot baby exercise spread like wildfire!

In no time at all, young ladies from all over, could be seen caring for a bot baby.

As it turned out, bot baby worked better for birth control than anything tried to date!

No one knew what happened to make Leon the way he was. If anyone tried to speak to him, he just mumbled........he could barely even feed himself!

AlaHanDrea was home brooding. "I should have absorbed him when I had the chance," she said out loud to herself...

———————————

Chapter 16

"Hey, AlaHanDrea, are you around? AlaHanDrea! Are you here?" Braynar called out. He was about to go down into his cave, when he saw air bubbles in the nearby pool.

"I should've known she was down there," he said out loud, to himself.

Braynar decided to take a moment and do something special for the teen queen...

When AlaHanDrea came out of the water, she was amazed at what she saw!

Someone had taken the trouble to put flowers in vases, a nice table by the water falls, rose peddles on the ground, pretty lace tablecloth on the table...

Nectar wine in goblets...

Pretty music was playing...

She smiled and used her magic to make herself look beautiful in anticipation of whoever and whatever ...

Braynar spotted her before she saw him. She looked so beautiful! He used his magic to make himself a bit more presentable...

He put on a tight button up shirt that really showed off his muscle tone..

His slacks also showed off his very muscular legs... Braynar was a big boy, for sure!

His muscles had muscles!

"Well, there you are, pretty lady."

"Bray! What..."

"Here, these roses are for you," Braynar told her.

"Thank you, Bray. They' re lovely!"

"AlaHanDrea, I have known you since the day you arrived on Taurus 9.

I have watched you grow up into a very beautiful young woman!

The truth is, well, the truth is..." She interrupted him... "You're interested in me romantically?"

"Woman! You drive me wild!

I can't stand the thought of you with another man while I stand idly by, waiting for you to get older...

You're plenty old enough right now! And I want you so badly,.... Woman.... "

He walked over and stood right in front of her, staring into her eyes... He bent down to kiss her and Sparks flew!

So, he kissed her more passionately.

She got Tingles up and down her spine as she melted into his arms.

AlaHanDrea wrapped her arms around him and kissed him back, igniting a fire deep inside of both of them...

It hadn't occurred to her that she could have Braynar, if she wanted him.

She'd always had a crush on him.

Her response was more than Braynar had hoped for.

"AlaHanDrea, can we go somewhere to be alone, just you and me?"

" We are alone," she replied.

"No, not like this." He shifted and had her climb on.

Braynar flew out over the sea... They were in the air for what seemed to be hours before spotting land.

When he said alone, he meant ALONE!

As they approached the island, Braynar let out loud screeches, alerting the natives to his presence. Then he flew in low to show off his passenger.

That was the first time she'd ever heard Braynar screech... He had such a deep voice and that screech was so high pitched!

As they approached the island, AlaHanDrea magically changed into warrior clothing and stood up as tho she were riding into battle...

Braynar let out more loud screeches, so AlaHanDrea let out her call, "yiyiyiyiyiyiyiyjyiyi!" Then waved down at the people.

He made one more pass, then headed up to the top of the highest mountain.

Much to AlaHanDrea's surprise, Braynar had a lair in there already!

As soon as they landed, he went over and struck the gong.

"Now, we are alone. The natives don't count," he told her.

"So, you mean alone, away from Keithen, Danalli, etc..."

"Well, right."

She giggled. "You want to play, you bad boy, and you don't want anyone to catch us!

You know that I'm still a virgin, right?"

"You mean to tell me that big kitty spent the night in your bed and did not make love to you?"

"That's exactly true. I wanted to, but he wouldn't. Instead, he made me do that whole bot baby thing."

"AlaHanDrea, what happened to Leon? He still has not recovered. I went by their den and he has guards on him like 24/7. He just sits there, mumbling incoherently. His parents are just beside themselves."

"I honestly don't know, Bray, we were fine, playing with bot baby, a storm was brewing, so, I went over to the hill....

After I finished the storm, I noticed a crowd around him, went to check it out and he freaked out on me as if I were some kind of monster! His mother made me leave and I haven't been back since."

"How strange. Leon fears nothing! He's one bad kitty! We all really like Leon. He's a fierce and brave warrior, that one. He'll make a fine king one day, but now, now he just sits and mumbles."

"Bray, we need to fix the Kitty! We can't just leave him like that. I really love Leon. We've been together since days after I was born! I brought him and his parents to Taurus 9... I love my lions... Bray, we've got to do something, but what?"

"You're in love with Leon?"

"I Love Leon, of course I Love Leon. What's not to love? I also love Keithen, Danalli, and Bray, I Love you, Too!

Y'all are my guys, my dudes!

I don't want to live in a world without you guys all in it!

And let's face it Bray, your smokin hot! All of you guys are smokin hot! I mean, smokin! I'd hate to have to choose just one!

He gabbed her and pulled her close, holding her snuggly... "Oh yeah? Well, what if I want to be first? I'm certified in Virgin detail, ya know."

"Braynar, you naughty dragon! You want to pick my flower..."

"You're damned straight I do!"

"And what if we make a baby?"

"AlaHanDrea, babies happen when sex happens. Sex is for making babies.."

"True, but having sex doesn't guarantee a baby will be made, it just means, well, that we went thru the motions and it could, may, maybe....."

"And if it does, would it be so bad? I'm a dragon, not a kitty. You'll lay an egg and I will carry it in my pouch.

I've already spoken to Healix. He tells me that you can do both, lay eggs and carry a child in your womb. The father determines live birth or egg.

I can't and won't get you pregnant. You will lay an egg and I do the rest."

"Oh really?"

"Yes, really. If I successfully fertilize an egg in you, you will lay that egg and I will put it in my pouch and do the rest. It's an added benefit to being with a dragon, girl." He giggled a little then flashed that gorgeous smile of his.

She put her arms around his neck, pulled herself up and kissed him very lovingly.

"So, what your telling me, is that you and I will be parents, could become parents, and you're cool with that?"

" Girl, I'd love nothing more than have children with you! How awesome will that be? What Incredible children they will be! AlaHanDrea, girl, I'm so much in love with you, you don't even know! I can be so gentle at first. I promise I won't hurt you.

"Braynar, I love the way it feels when you kiss me.

I love the way you feel.

I never realized that being together with you was even an option.

I love being allowed to touch you, to taste you, to experience you... I'm not used to being able to touch a man's body, and Bray, baby, you have got one hell of a body, dude, You are so fine!"

"I never realized you thought so. I never knew you wanted me like that."

"I used to day dream about you and I being together, when I was just kid.

I know nothing of how to pleasure a man.

Yes, I do know where the penis goes, that's not what I mean.

I mean, I don't really even know much of what a penis looks like!

I got to see the kitties penis when I used magic to remove his pants, but he used magic to put them right back on again. And he's a kitty. You're a dragon. I suspect they look differently?"

"You worry too much. I can give you a biology lesson, or, I can just show you as we go. But we talk too much." He said, then scooped her up in his arms and carried her into his lair.

He took her over to a lounge, laid her down on it and before she could even say a word, be pinned her arms down over her head, then attached shackles to her wrists and ankles!

"Braynar, what are you doing? Ok I can get out , you know, if I want to?"

"Oh, you can, can you? Go ahead, give it a try." He said, smugly
.

She wiggled around, struggled some, then struggled a lot! She even tried to pop out or use magic to free herself, but soon discovered that she really was at Braynar's mercy!

"Braynar, baby, how did you manage to make it to where I can't get free?"

"I'm a strong and powerful dragon, sweetheart!

I'm even powerful for one such as you!

Inside my lair, inside this lair in particularly, my power is the only power that counts.

You are now mine to do with as I choose... Does that scare you?"

"Should it?"

"Probably, yes. It should, but does it? "

"Truthfully?

Yes, a little."

Her clothes vanished. Braynar stood, staring at her in all of her glory, admiring the beauty of her.

She laid there, unsure of what to do.

The situation was strangely tantalizing...

Braynar used his magic to put a full white gown on her. It was very sheer, but covered her, just the same.

Then, he shifted to dragon state.

That's when she began to get nervous... Braynar was a very fierce dragon! He could eat her in one bite and she knew it!

What she didn't know, was why he shifted to dragon state!

Much to her surprise, he turned and left the cave, leaving her bound to that lounge.

Fireplaces lit as he left the cave.

She began to shiver and blankets appeared on her lounge, as did soft pillows.

Sweet, gentle music began playing and before she knew it, she had fallen asleep.

Hours passed.

Night came.

She slept.

Morning came, still she slept.

When she finally woke up, there was a potty chair next to the lounge and the chains were longer. Once she had finished with the chair, it vanished.

2 large bowls of hot water and one of cool water sat on a table with soap and towels. After she was through washing, food appeared. Regular food like humans ate.

When her meal was compete, the mess vanished.

But no Braynar.

A screen appeared on the wall near the first fireplace. A fictional movie began playing on it.

She had never really been one to watch a movie before, so that was a treat.

Once the movie was over, the cave became very quiet.

A lunch tray appeared on the table and when she was done, it vanished also.

Another movie played, then another ...

Another meal appeared, so, she ate it and just like before, the mess vanished.

More movies played. On about the third one, she dozed off.

Morning came and was exactly like the day before.

She couldn't figure out why Braynar tricked her and imprisoned her the way he had.

Tears rolled down her cheeks as she thought about being tricked and imprisoned like that.

She had thought Braynar was telling her the truth and really wanted to be with her.

It was easy to forget that the guys were dragons. They were not ever even partly human or humanoid.

Being human was an illusion.

A tool for hiding themselves...

She questioned herself as to why she even trusted the beasts...

She didn't even have her mother with her anymore!

Time lost all meaning as the days and nights blended...

Braynar had really brought her to an obscure place!

What possible reason could he have had to want to lock her away in an isolated cave?

She went over their entire conversations with a fine toothed comb.

The only thing she could think of was Leon.

Then, it came to her. Why hadn't she thought of it before!

Of course!

Such a simple explanation!

She wasn't really imprisoned in a cave!

She was in her own mind! She had to be!

She just had to be!

"AlaHanDrea!

AlaHanDrea!

It's Isabel.

Can you hear me?

Baby girl, can you hear me?"

"AlaHanDrea! Baby girl, it's me, Athena! Where are you?"

"AlaHanDrea! Can you hear me? Baby girl, where are you?" Isabel was trying hard to reach the teen queen. "I'm not reaching her!" Isabel cried.

"Neither am I," Athena said, worry in her voice.

"AlaHanDrea, it's me baby, it's Danalli. Baby girl, please, answer me!"

"DaNalli! Oh Danalli! Where are you? I can't see you! Help me Danalli, please help me! I'm imprisoned ... Braynar did it! I'm on an island? Help! Please hurry! Help me, Danalli, Please get me out of here!!"

"AlaHanDrea, try to summon me.... This is Danalli, baby, focus, I believe you've been drugged! Please, baby girl, now, focus and summon me!"

"Danalli!" she cried out.

"Yes, baby girl, oh yes, I can hear you now! Listen to me, focus! Summon me to you!"

"Isabel, I almost had her! She said she's in a mountain on an island and that Braynar imprisoned her!"

"Braynar?" Isabel was shocked. "Isn't it possible that she's having delusions?"

"I'm sure anything's possible..." Danalli replied.

"Danalli, we have got to find her! We need to find Braynar and make him take us to her!" Isabel ordered.

"Your majesty, we can't find Braynar either..." Jason, her new member of the guard, told her.

"Danalli! Danalli! Where did you go?" AlaHanDrea cried. "Danalli! You come here this instance! Oh Danalli, my magic doesn't work in here! Help me please, Danalli please! Help me!" She cried.

"Isabel, I think I know where she is! She said her magic doesn't work there... Braynar has a cave on an island in the South Seas. There's a special ore in the mountain that could be restricting her ability to use her magic... I'm flying down there right now, would you like to come with me? It's a long flight," Danalli asked Isabel.

"Well, C'mon, let's go!" Isabel said as she was taking to the air.

The flock saw her and Danalli take off and flew out after them.

It was truly a site to behold!

Over a thousand dragons flew across the ocean following their queen....

Everyone of them determined to locate the missing teen queen....

She'd been missing for way too long...

Isabel suddenly stopped in mid air!

She had telepathically told George what was going on and George had just told her that Braynar had been with him!

Then, George told her to continue going there to look..... While him, Braynar, Keithen and Thomlin were on their way to join them!

Danalli continued to call out to AlaHanDrea when he suddenly vanished!

Isabel didn't know the way without Danalli!. But there was no where to land!

Danalli was able to telepathically contact Isabel as well as the flock...

"Baby girl was finally able to summon me... I'm with her now ... I can't open the shackles holding her! Stay on the course you are on, Isabel, then go 20 degrees south by Southeast. You'll see the island. The tallest peak on the tallest mountain, N by NW 7 degrees... follow my signal..."

"We're on our way!" Isabel messaged him.

George and his whole crew were quickly catching up with the flock!

Dragons had excellent honing skills that worked better than a GPS!

Their ability to telepathically speak to one another, or the whole flock at one time, was one of their most valued assets... Communication being the key to success in all areas of life.

George sent a message for everyone to follow him. King Neptune cleared a spot in the sea of all large predators so the dragons could safely land on the water.

The entire flock sat down quietly and un noticed... It was as if they had fallen from the air and Vanished from sight.

Whales swam up to assist the dragons... When they showed up, a couple of dozen dragon busted out laughing so hard they could barely swim...it only took a minute for everyone to realize what had them laughing so hard... The rest of the flock fell over laughing as well...

They were remembering attacking the pirates and AlaHanDrea saying that she didn't swallow sea men....even the whales got a laugh over that one.

Danalli was back in the cave, and he even began laughing at the memories, when he heard the rest of them...

"What's so damned funny? She asked.

"Baby girl, do you remember when we went to get rid of the pirates?"

"Well, of course I do, what did I say that everyone found so damned funny?"

"Oh, my sweet, precious girl ..." Once Danalli explained it to her, she laughed so hard, she almost peed herself!

"I still can't get these damned chains to release," Danalli said in frustration.

"Danalli, this is Braynar. The real Braynar. I'm on my way. Don't let the imposter catch you there, he will try to kill you! I put a wreath around my neck. Your magic won't work in there. Bro, hide yourself, NOW!"

"AlaHanDrea, act like I'm not here. He is not Braynar! Braynar has a wreath on his neck, now shhh."

AlaHanDrea laid down and faked sleeping.

The fake Braynar entered the cave. "I'm sorry that I've been gone so long, baby girl. I ran into a bit of trouble."

"I've been so worried!" she replied.

"I'm so sorry. I really didn't mean to leave you chained up in a cave on a remote island."

"Didn't you, tho? I mean, it's the whole reason you brought me here... To imprison me. I don't get why you dressed me in a sheer gown, tho, only to leave me alone."

"Truthfully, I was actually sent to kill you. But I couldn't do that. Not after kissing you. I don't know what to do now."

"Who are you? What are you?" she asked.

"I'm half mimic, half dragon. I'm sorry I drugged you. Those who sent me, think I threw you into the volcano. They think you are dead. They will kill my family if you live," he explained.

"But, who wants me dead?" she asked.

"The Pirates. They want you, Braynar, Keithen, George, Isabel and Danalli dead. They plan to feed your dragons to the ichneumons!" He admitted.

"Oh they do, do they?" Braynar said as he entered the lair, with George, Keithen and Thomlin.

The mimic/dragon dropped to the ground, bowing before them.

"Release her, now!" George ordered.

"Yes, your majesty."

Danalli came out of the dark, took AlaHanDrea in his arms like a baby and left with her, headed for Drakonia. Isabel saw them and joined them. A small Entourage followed them for safety, while the remainder of the flock stayed with George.

The mimic/dragon, Stephen, had his powers bound and was placed in a cage. While the dragons readied for battle.

King Neptune was furious! The fleet of Pirates were anchored off the coast of the central island. King Neptune rose up out of the deep, swelled to giant size in obvious fury! Creatures from the sea gathered below the ships ...

The Dragons took to the air, surrounding the island! The pirates trembled in fear as they released the family of mimic/dragons as ordered. A small group of dragons took Stephen and his family and sent them to mimic island, while the remaining dragons landed on the island, killing every pirate the natives had not already killed!

King Neptune caused the sea to turn the ships over, feeding all aboard to his awaiting creatures.

When the day was through, not one pirate survived.

The Islanders threw a celebration party for the dragons as well as the creatures from the sea.

The islands population stood staring in utter disbelief, while sea creatures shifted to human state, walking up out of the sea to party and celebrate with them...

The islands chief was so grateful for being rid of those cut throat pirates, he raised a Drakonian flag, declaring the island as the property of Drakonia, forever more under the protection of the dragons!

King George stood tall, with his son's proudly at his side, while everyone bowed to their ruling king...

Don't miss out!

Visit the website below and you can sign up to receive emails whenever Jeri Andrew publishes a new book. There's no charge and no obligation.

https://books2read.com/r/B-A-YGIAB-JUDOC

BOOKS2READ

Connecting independent readers to independent writers.

About the Author

Retired, I now spend my time writing stories from my imagination, to share with others, to help carry them away to another world, a world of magic and intrigue...